FACT OF FATE

FACT OF FATE

Digambar Muni Pranamya Sagar

PRABHAT
PAPERBACKS

Published by
PRABHAT PAPERBACKS
4/19 Asaf Ali Road,
New Delhi-110 002 (INDIA)
e-mail: prabhatbooks@gmail.com

ISBN 978-93-5266-577-8
FACT OF FATE
by Digambar Muni Pranamya Sagar

Edition
First, 2018

Price
₹ 250.00 (Rupees Two Hundred Fifty only)

Printed at
Deep Colour Scan Pvt. Ltd., Delhi

About the Author

Muni Shri 108 Pranamya Sagar Ji is one of the great Digambar Jain Saint. He is one of the saints who is trying his best to motivate Jain as well as the Non-Jain community. He is a great Indian Poet & Writer. He belongs to Aacharya Shri Vidhyasagar Ji Maharaj's Disciples of learners. His writing skills are very appealing and heart touching.

In his writings, we always get something new. He inspires youngsters through his speech and compositions. His endeavour is to make the association as strong as possible. Digambar Muni Pranamya Sagar is one of the most learned saints, a well known unconventional Digambar monk, a master of unique talent as an author, a hardened Saadhak, a master of Sanskrit, Hindi, Prakrit & English who has composed many Sanskrit, Hindi and English texts. Now he has composed a new literature naming **"Fact of Fate"**, for the sake of humanity & general interest, in which he has given a new way, a new direction of living life.

The Arham Meditation Yoga Saadhak has written 45 books till now based on moral values, humanity, religion, education and many more. In this book, Maharaj Shri has mentioned solutions of each and every problem which we are facing nowadays.

The Young Jain Saint has crossed all the barriers of social systems and proved that no one has seen a more saintly figure than him in recent times. He is the powerful one amongst all the saints to walk on the path of the monarchy. I can say that he is like a huge tree working for the betterment and uplift of the society religiously, educationally, socially. He teaches every person living in the society to do some effort for the development of the society.

One of his book Lakshya aims to bring today's youth to the right direction so that they can achieve their aim effectively. It contains small stories from which one can understand the difference between good-bad, dharma-adharma, sin-chastity. This book conveys the aim of life while another book of Maharaj Ji i.e. **"Life Management In View Of Lord Mahavira"** teaches us 'Live & Let Live'. It is available on Amazon.com as well. He gave a new form of Yoga and Meditation. His book Arham Yoga and Meditation has also been published.

Now he has composed this book i.e. FACT OF FATE, which is revealing the Mantra of living Life in a right manner, especially for youngsters.

Devotees.

India has been called 'VISHWA GURU' since times immemorial. This credit is given to India because of spiritual heights shown by our saints and sages. These divine souls are the lighthouse who enlighten and guide the people to move ahead on the right path.

Digambar Saint Muni Pranamya Sagar is one of the noble souls who has been a spiritual Guru, writer, poet, reformer and the ambassador of 'ARHAM YOGA'. Muni Shri has been motivating the students of various institutions for excelling in their fields. He gives them tips for controlling pressure and tension of education. He has been inspiring the people through different 'ARHAM YOG CAMPS' about healthy lifestyle and how people can cure incurable diseases through this Yoga practice. He is also the saviour of our old Prakrit Language. During his **'Chaturmas'** at Rewari, he taught prakrit language to many teachers and students. This is really a commendable service to our culture and tradition.

I am really grateful to the Almighty God for providing me the opportunity of meeting Muni Shri. I think this is the part of sheer divine planning for giving me such a good opportunity of doing some translation work. It was really a very good experience. I came across many new ideologies and philosophies and for their explanation, I met Muni Shri. He explained them in a very simple and impressive manner. I feel very motivated and blessed.

Though I have tried to translate some articles according to my capabilities, being a humble poor soul, I may not have reached up to the best level. I beg pardon for this. I pray to the Almighty God for more such opportunities in life!!!

A Seeker of Blessings

Contents

1
Fact of Fate

This question arises in mind of every genius. We can't tell you the answer to this question according to the religious and mythological literature. If we ask about this to our friends and intellectuals, we will find different answers and different views.

If you ask this question to a physically disabled, the reply will be to be a physically good. If you are inquiring regarding this to a sick the reply will be to free from diseases. If you ask the same question to a disfigured, the reply will be to be pretty.

If the same query will be asked for a menial, the answer will come to be a superior one. If you interrogate about this to a child, the answer will be to become an engineer or a doctor. When you are querying the same to an unemployed, the answer will be to get a job. If you will ask this to an employed, the reply will be prosperity.

If you will ask the same to a rich, the answer will be to become a leader and from a leader, the reply will be to be influential. We observe that everyone wants to fulfill his desire.

Therefore the fact of fate lies in the fulfillment of mental wishes and enormous expectations. If one accomplishes his desires with less effort or an early age, he thinks destiny stands at other doors.

Really destiny is the manifestation of our past karmas. No one knows what will happen to the next moment. Someone has a favorable atmosphere with family, society, kith, and kin. Consequently, he becomes a man of great importance with less effort in any field of any kind like sports, business, job, politics, and socialism. Such a person is a person with a bright fortune.

On the other hand, someone who has an unfavorable atmosphere with family, society, kith, and kin, he gradually becomes a man of less strength and effect in all fields of activity and responsibility. Such a person is a person with low fortune. Most of the people had no clear sign of good and bad luck. They have a better chance of success because of their feasible mentality with a firm attitude. They also have a tendency to bring a sudden change in themselves, even in fearsome conditions. They are laborious, diligent and gracious in whole life without paying attention to luck. Such kind of people have luck in their own hands and have the power to change the world around them.

Think that you are lucky because you have five senses which are more than other creatures. You have extra power to do anything that you like, more than animals and birds. You also have a sense of good thinking more than other men. Whenever you are in misery and feel frustration and destruction, never think to destroy your life. You have eyes to see far in the sky. You have two arms to do hard work. You have two legs to go ahead. You have a best and vast mind to think good and act positively. It's all your fate. Under any circumstances never try to commit suicide. If you blame your fate, it means you are an enemy of your own. Fate increases using the power what you gained. It is the fact of fate.

□

2
To Overcome Fear

In the habit of every living being, we can observe that the four tendencies are common in all. Food eating, fear, Sexual interest and to collect things. Except fear all the three factors have a desire to take something. Fear can be of outer things and also of inner unnecessary feelings. Fear generates when we want to have something, when we want to fulfill our desire, when we think what will happen tomorrow.

The first letter of fear is F which denotes Failure; it means lack of intelligence. Everybody wants to get success. If one is unfamiliar with the circumstances that are possible in that field, definitely he will be afraid. Your aim should be clear and should also be fully devoted to that. Sometimes we take a risk for profit because we know **"No risk no gain"**. In this case, our opinion and purpose must be beneficial to all with honesty and validity. Whenever you choose a new field, oppositions and difficulties might be faced. We have to overcome all these with patience and without any fear. It is the only way to win the fever of fear. In case of failure think that it is the way of success. Realizing that what will you do if not succeed.

F

The second letter of Fear is E – Enmity, more the number of enemies the more the degree of fear in mind, one who squash and use a threat is also threatened like Napoleon. Adverse attitude and misunderstanding behavior are also the root cause of enmity. One is never afraid of anybody and he never gets afraid of any even he had no weapon. So to overcome the feelings of fear control feelings and avoid hostility. Enmity means misconception about others. This emotion weakens our own spiritual level and slowly and slowly converts the positive energy of mind into negative. At last, the mind becomes an enemy of himself.

E

The third letter of fear is A – Abusive. Activities, like Speaking abusively language and beating others, are the cause of Fear. A person who commits moral mistakes, emotional black mailing, sexual assaults, indecisive statement, falls in negative energy and then he gets fearful. If you have not performed ugly wordings and arguments to others than you will be in a fearless state of mind. Like this, if anyone says you abusing words listen to them peacefully. Always think that the wordings are only non-conscious matter touched with our ears and go away. Use of proper sweety words shows the inner awareness of anyone.

A

The fourth letter of Fear R says Regretting when we continuously think about the loss of anything or anybody. We are surrounded by fear of emotions. My father has died, my parents didn't have too much money, I have no friend, No one is getting friendly with me and so on. So when our mind focuses on the regret of the past, we are in fear. Once a girl student came to me and asked How she could overcome her fear. I asked her – What type of fear do you have? She said– **"My mother bothers with the disease of white marks on her body. I am worried to think that the same disease may not happen to my body."** So when our mind focuses on future we are in fear. So to be free from fear, concentrate your mind on the present moment only.	**R**

The word 'FEAR' also denotes the solution itself.

F- Face it under any circumstances.

E- Enthusiastic

A-Awareness

R- Release it.

It means – Face it Enthusiastically and with awareness and release it.

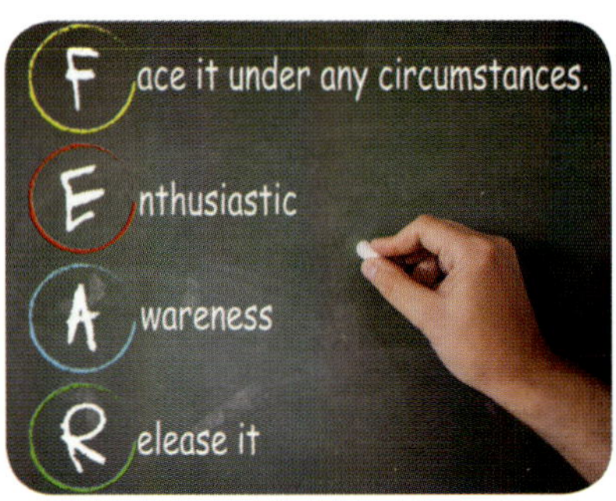

□

3
Life With Love

Love means not to expect anything from anyone. Everyone wants either Love or to be loved. Love is an act of doing, not desiring. Love is not done by thinking of a choice. Love is an inner attribute of the soul. It expresses deep satisfaction and bliss. It is not dependable and demanding quality. Depending attributes manifesto our quality for some time. Any pure attribute like love can never be banished. As the sun always loves lotus without touching, demanding and desiring anything so natural and independents pure love.

More attachment to indulgences falls into hatred. You would have seen deeper and sticking relations between two brothers, two friends, two lovers which often turn into hatreds and harassment and ends in departure, divorce or suicide. So love is which gives us sweetness or sorrows initially and bitter grief at last. It is not loving, but attraction.

Love is an attribute of soul. So more you like one self more you get bliss and satisfaction without any dependency on others. On the other hand affection depends on relation made by physical attraction.

Lord Mahavira has loved all living beings of the Universe. So, Why he has been loved by everyone? Lord Mahavira always loved his own soul, without seeing, talking and desiring others for twelve years. It is a penance to love every creature of three worlds. Saints and seers also live in self. So they are also loved by all. Meditation, chanting, and silence living make a way of love. So by-pass over this world by these ways.

□

4

Kayotsarga—A Breathing Meditation

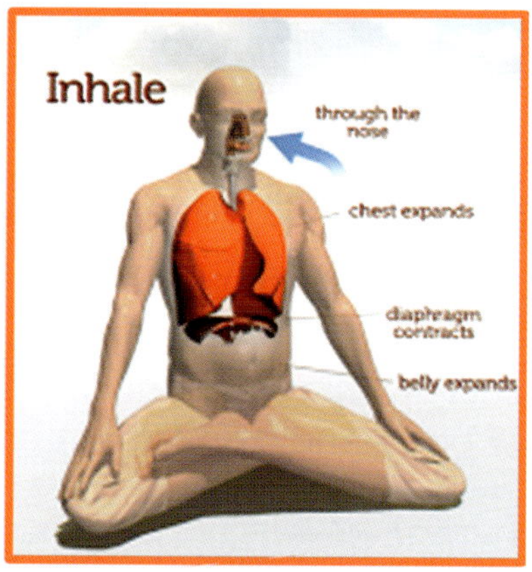

Austerities followed by monks have seemed very hard when they are connected do physical body only. But these seem very easy when connected with beyond the bodily nature. There are two types of Austerities one is Outer which depends on the physical body and the other is Internal which depends on mind and soul. External Austerities are very effective and the root cause of the destruction of past Karmas, also change the level of the conscious mind and first give the feelings of harmony and peace. One of them is Kayotsarga- means detachment of Kaya (body) by breathing concentration. When we concentrate on our mind in breathing process, it becomes meditation.

One Kayotsarga has twenty-seven (27) counts of breathing. Inhaling and exhaling is one complete breath. While inhaling utter OM and at the time of exhaling speak ARHAM. So count 27 times breathing in one Kayotsarga. Observe how our mind targets all types of negative emotions like worry, anxiety, depression, fear, etc. We can perform it anytime, at any place. Whenever we want to be free from outer world's stress. Whenever we want to relax, whenever we want to meditate, we can perform gently one Kayotsarga. If, we have some more time we can do second Kayotsarga. By this process, we gradually realize that what is permanent in this cover. When we close our eyes and observe the breath with counting, we feel completely detached from living world associated with the five senses.

At that time body lives completely in nature and collect an enormous amount of cosmic energy. That energy increases the immunity and resistance level of body and mind that gives you increased resistance level of the body which gives you the pleasure of the healthy and disease free body.

On the other hand, the increased resistance level of mindset makes you free from the fear of insecurity, jealousy, competition, and safety. It seeds a permanent, solid and stable nature of the soul. The soul is the real source of joy and happiness. Kayotsarga can be performed in sitting or standing position. It is completely like Yoga, Nidra i.e. sleep without lying. Jain monks do this Kayotsarga for a long time and feel oneness with one. Bahubali had done this Kayotsarg for one year in standing position and his father Lord Rishabdeva did it for six months in sitting position. That's the story of prehistoric time, but today we can do this for a short time as long as possible. By this process, we will feel that we live beyond the living nature and the material world.

So do this meditation without any condition of the place, weather and religious rituals.

□

5

Reality of God

Who is God? What is the work of God? What is God doing for us? What have we got from God? What happens to soul when one becomes God? God is one or infinite. When do you say he is really God?

It is important to know the answer of these questions. Otherwise one cannot get right knowledge. Before knowing who is God, first try to know what's the work of God.

- *May God is doer of this world, our body, our relatives, our pains & pleasures of God. Does he work for all the infinite beings and what does he get after doing this?*

- *Is it possible for God to have a list of work of every living being? Scientists do not agree about the existence of God.*
- *Iron law, the immutable Law of cause and effect is working in this Universe naturally. Everything happens according to this law in the cosmos the living beings like men, deities, animals or non-living beings like table, tree, house, crops, book etc....*

Everything is doing its own work with self potency. A modern scientist Dr. Stephen Hawking said that this universe is not made by God, it functions itself. According to the law of cause and effect, it functions according to the law of energy, which says that energy can not be created or destroyed but it changes its form from one to another. Keeping these two laws in mind you can get answer of every question, you can solve every problem of your mind and you can get really true knowledge.

These laws are working for all the living beings. So 'What you sow, you will reap'. Today you are in that position which you sow in the past. You are getting fruits of your own deeds. And now what you are sowing, you will reap that in the future. It's also the law of cause and effect. The same law is applicable for non-living beings as well. It can also be defined by Action and Reaction i.e. Newton's third law is also fitted in every working, which clearly says that God is not the doer of this work, he is not working for us.

Now we have to remember that we are not the shadow of any supreme or not the part of anyone. We are completely on our own. We are not due to others, we have our own thoughts and bliss. We can get everything desirable in this way, logically not by chance. So God is also a free entity of this Universe like us. The difference is that he is free from all the distortions, opposite and negative emotions, thoughts and also free from the body.

□

6

Experience is Life

Most of us are studying various subjects from childhood to old age, in the course of each type of study. We first learn, then we take the test. It is the life of school and college, but our actual life is associated with our family and society with a variety of responsibilities. It needs our intelligence which is more important than any type of degree achieved in our schools and colleges.

Intelligence means how you face problems of the life, how much time do you take to be normal after adverse situations. You feel mental disturbance or not in any critical situation. This type of intelligence comes from experience. So experience in life is not accumulation of information. We find experience through the trials in any criteria, without risk and trial there is no experience.

So without an experience, there is no life because an experience is a life. If we are afraid of such types of experiences, it means we are afraid of life. As a common human being we all are afraid of an initiative, why do we depend on the experience of others. Why are we so much interested in listening other's life story which becomes an idol for others. For this, we have to face experiences in our life. You know the mathematics of experience is just opposite of study.

In case of experience, you have to take test first and learn later. In this case, you don't know what will happen after this risk. Maybe successful or unsuccessful, may be good or bad, may be better or bitter, may be rich or poor. If you are ready for anything then life is very simple and enjoyable.

When life will be full of experiences, then you will automatically realize what's the source of life. So be ready for test and learn other lessons of life. How sad! We have to read lesson first and then test our whole life. So this mentality is the obstacle in living a happy life.

□

7

All are Same: When?

Every person in this world is unique. He desires to be an extraordinary person, having things like clothes, pets, house, service & even his wife. We always search something extra hidden in every ordinary thing. Everybody wants to see the extraordinary picture, wants to listen to the amazing statement, and wants to think in an extraordinary way, so that he becomes the object of everyone. As long as, this method plays in our mind we can never recognize reality. We will never feel the peace of mind and real bliss of soul. We will be far away from spirituality. You will be blind to yourself. It is called illusion and fullness according to right knowledge. A spiritual man is one who is really satisfied with his simplicity. He becomes more and more animated. As water in its original state, as air in the unseen state, as the smell of flower with nature. He wants nothing all owing in his mind from outside. He tries to get free from all emotions and physical attachment.

If you try to go deeper within, outer world seems like a wood with no sensation. This inner feeling is the beginning of spirituality. You will feel that you love yourself, you will feel lightened with mind and delighted in divine soul. If you have fear of this process, you may not feel what you are. With the real point of view, the soul of everyone is in ordinary state. The soul has no colour, no smell, no touch, no sound, no taste. To love that ordinary stage of the true love of soul and devotion to the God. A yogi lives in such a state. He directs all his energy to that divine world, so he naturally becomes celibate. He becomes truly, honest with himself. He is really a saint. He does not need clothes and has no barrier of the social system. He always feels free from lust, anger, ego and all types of extraordinary feelings of love. A person of real personality has sensitivity and for him all are same.

□

8
My Nature

Everyone remembers the dignified personality. Everyone makes an image of the icon in his mind. What the nobleman has notable, it is not worthy of us and others. Every important person is filled with very simple qualities. If we think about Ram, Mahavir and others we will find they were really attached to reality. They all lived freely in all situations and circumstances.

They were recognised as the mystery of this universe. So they stopped fighting and resisting to any one or anything. All the people get the fruits of their own Karmas that they had seeded in past life.

They have no idea what is going to happen at next moment. Ram and such personalities believe in the Karma Philosophy deeply. Ram was very happy at that time to go into the forest as he lived in his kingdom. Neminath diverted his path suddenly after seeing the dance of cruelty for his marriage. Good and bad feelings are also the result of our own Karmas.

Karma is not our own nature. My nature is beyond the outcome of these karmas. Have a tendency to accept all that has happened in our life. Never blame others. Always think that I am the only one responsible for my good and bad conditions.

No one else is included in my life doing good or bad even God and Guru. This thinking leads to the fulfillment of your heart with harmony and love for all. Remember that Ram never commented on his mother 'KAIKAY' and his father 'DASHRATH'. He had no anguish with his Brother 'BHARAT' when he got the whole kingdom. He was also not in distress when he lost his beloved wife 'SITA'.

□

9

Educational View

Our Nation as a whole is a nation of different regional and local languages with the national language Hindi. In 1835, first Macaulay had introduced English in Indian education system to make all nations English internally. It was a deceiving trick to change nationality and to make mental slaves. We are seeing that Macauly is now eighty percent successful in his long-range mission. Now in this the age of globalization, everyone is interconnected with the help of internet and it is impossible to discard the learnings and teachings of English completely.

All around there are two types of people with two types of thoughts about English. The first thinks that English is the language of the whole nation. It is now much more necessary to teach and learn our children in English medium. Many management gurus, high profile celebrities and masters of education system always promote the English medium based education. They know that their kids can increase the percentage of earning at every step of their life. Their kids can get high standard jobs in reputed companies. They admit them in private colleges paying large scale fees. The reality is that despite all this, they never give them a view of global success and personal peace, cultural values, a wide thinking in literature, science and sociality. As a result of this, the students and entrants are becoming elites and entities who consider others inferior.

We have seen an example of this when a central minister says that we can not travel by cattle class people (general department in a train). Also, they have no knowledge of local language mixed with familiar meanings of words like Jwar, Bazara, Kadhi, Lachaka, Bari etc. eatable things like Daal, Bhaat, Bakhara etc. have natural names and they do not know several names of common things like bottle gourd which is also called Loki, Ghiya, Aaal. etc. in different regions. So lack of knowledge of our ethnical etymology is a major drawback of English education.

Second, the section of second class people who know the importance of our Hindi language as a language of the nation. They are worried about English as it is competing and destroying vernacular. After that, they also admit their children in English medium schools to make them deserved.

Nowadays, the education does not depend on the personal interest seeing an advantage disadvantage of culture, language, and traditional factors. But it also depends on the salary and status of a person. It depends also on the atmosphere surrounding you. We can never see a person who has such loyalty to our nation that he is living a prosperous and lucky life, and leads his kids to study in Hindi medium.

We need to have both Hindi and English respectively like mother and wife. Our mind is like a lighted and Airfree home. In this, Hindi is necessary just as the main gate. At the same time, English or other languages work like windows. Without doors, there is no image of a good home. Also, windows in houses are important too and provide convenience.

A far from the opposition, we should accept easily the importance of both languages. Never think that English is the only ultra most uttered world class famous language. In the language survey, it was found the second grade in the world. The first is Chinese and the third one is Hindi. So be proud to be an Indian and of this Indian language.

The most Ancient Indian language is Prakrit contemporary to Sanskrit. The words of so many regional languages are also heard up to this time. So, we also have a responsibility to save the Prakrit, the Grand Ma of all the languages in the world. Basic Jain scriptures, Buddha scriptures, and many historical plays are written in Prakrit language.

"Prakrit is our Grand Ma,
Sanskrit is our Grand Pa,
Hindi is our Mother,
Apbhransha is our Father,
And English is our Wife."

□

10

Secret of Eternal Happiness

A soul is full of eternal bliss. Please try to realize it and feel it. True happiness doesn't lie in the fulfillment of our wants. True happiness is independent of everything and every other person. AACHARYA PUJYAPAD said - **AATMANUSHTHAN NISHTHASYA.** Paramanand by the experience of the true soul. So try to experience and feel it at all times without any condition. This Paramanad burns all the mental worries and psyche disturbances. This Paramanand enables the heart to feel happiness in any action whether it is related to eating, walking, talking, reading, teaching or in meditation, pray etc. A yogi always set up his mind doing everything for his soul. He eats for his soul because after eating he gets energy into his body and this energy again works to experience his bliss of soul. The mutual transformation of energy leads to staying much more time in a state of true happiness.

So by this process, physical energy converts into internal energy. This energy conversion process continues in Yogi's life till he attains complete bliss, called NIRVANA.

A real Saint feels happy when he extirpates his hairs with his hands, when he does fast for a day, 2 or 3 and so on, when he doesn't see beautiful women, when he performs austerity freely and independently.

JAIN ACHARYA also said that- The pain of performing austerities themselves is better than the enjoyment which depends on others. So the path of a soul is completely independent of other outer objects. It is really a state of self-discipline. This secret of eternal happiness is much more valuable than any other worldly objects like money, land, job, wife, and business.

□

11

Live With Love

Love is the very nature of our soul. Love is the natural and normal power existing in all living beings. It is the source of all sorts of bliss what we want to accomplish. Love is the external power of a kind full heart. Love is above all the desirable things such as wealth and abundance. It is the liberty of a meaningful life. Love is the relationship with all creatures.

Before this, have you ever thought How essential love is? What you think when you hear the word 'Love'? Can you measure the range of love and emotions? Do you know how a person becomes beloved for all? Such a special quality also exists within us. We should live with love. There is a little difference between 'To Live' and 'To Love'.

If we see the spelling, we find when "I" is replaced by "o", then live converts into love. 'I' stands for "pride" or "ego". We all live with various types of egos.

LIVE - I + O = L♥VE

I am a doctor, engineer, best poet, best writer, industrialist, businessman and also a saint. Everyone in any respect is deeply cocky. If this 'I' will be removed from us, we will be same from inside as well as outside. The soul will become as natural as nature. Our all expressions and activities will be full of kindness and that is surely pure love. "I" can be removed by 'O'. 'O' means only to come at the stage of oneness. We should adopt obliging nature. As far as one obliges, one gets the quality of being obedient. Dwindling of 'I' based emotions manifests true nature of your own.

Love is not only a matter of exposition but a deep and serene penance. Nowadays this holy word has lost its pure meaning. Lust is a general emotion which is present in all living beings including birds, animals, hell and heaven beings. Love produced in the heart when the lust becomes null and void in mind. Lust is always present in unconscious mind. Only a yogi can win this lust by controlling his five senses with spiritual knowledge.

In the absence of this lust, the soul experiences the real friendship with everyone in nature. This state of soul is called Reality. The soul becomes real godlike Thirthankar, adorable to all men and deity. This sexual desire with opposite sex body or the similar sex body dwelled in soul from the beginning less time. So the opposite of lust is true love.

Feelings of love without affection and sexual desires come in one's mind by the repeated process of likeness and loveliness of oneself. It is not even easy to control for a monk or yogi. Whenever you want to see, touch, talk, walk continuously and suddenly with a woman, you have no feelings of love with reality. These desires are also the presentation of ill will about a woman. A monk or yogi can observe within self-love or lust by observing his thinking about appetite. Anyone who loves himself and has a craving to see his pure soul by taking renouncement from worldly pleasure can feel true love. This pattern triggers in you as a feeling of god and a form of happiness with calmness.

□

12
Traditional Truth

Traditional activities are scientific. If they are related to religious saints and muni. We should think about them, sincerely and seriously. We are discussing here one of them that why Jain saints eat with hands only. This tradition is not only for saints and monks but for Indian householders also to eat with hands. Nowadays this experience and its virtues have been proved by gastronomic art also.

Eating food with our hands feeds not only our body but also our mind and the spirit. We can see this culture in India in every city and state, even in villages, up to the time when hotels were not everywhere. During weddings and other celebrations, people ate food with the use of their fingers instead of using fork and spoon.

Once I went to a hotel with my friends to eat 'Dosa' at the time when I was not a saint. I started eating without using a fork. They looked at me with a slight smile and told to pierce, cut and raise with cutlery and then to eat. I was surprised but at that moment I felt it was the proper way to eat this 'special dish otherwise people will think as a rustic. Like me, many Indians accepted this style of living without scrutiny.

Actually, this eating style belongs to fleshly obese persons. We see when any Indian eats the tasty food he tastes by taking his fingers into his mouth, again and again, licking his fingers. In an article of Tarun Basu we read – **"The Ayurvedic texts teach that each finger is an extension of one of the five elements. The Thumb is Agni (fire) – you might have seen children**

sucking their thumb when they are unable to chew. The forefinger is Vayu (air). The Middle Finger is Akash (ether – the tiny intercellular spaces in the human body), the ring finger is Prithivi (Earth) and the little finger is Jal (water)."

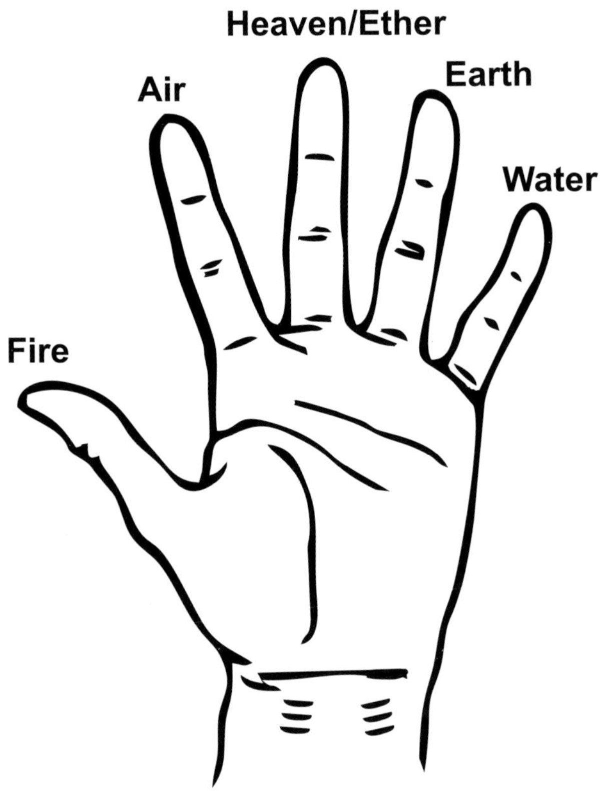

□

13
You are Unique

Nothing is equal in this world neither matter nor soul. You see the face of so many people and no one is similar. By birth, we are definitely different from others. We are different in the sense of color, beauty, Knowledge, expressions, liking, testing, seeing, speaking, temperaments and activities. The working of a body is different for every individual and this holds true even in case of twins. Why does this happen? It is not only in case of mankind but one finds the similar difference in the animal beings. One can think that two cows are similar in appearance, two birds are alike by face, two monkeys are same by eyes but they are also different from human beings. Animals also look at human beings and find them similar, just as human beings see animals. 'Why are they not similar to others?' Put this question in regular practice and the question will become answer automatically when you will be in perfect consciousness. The answer is you are unique in this world. You are only you and no one is like you. Do not compare yourself to anyone.

The comparison is the process of degrading your own values because it is the cause of all types of sorrows, grief, depression, and anxiety. It is the phenomena of

'Dharma' that every entity in this universe has its own existence and to live with our existence is potentiality.

So many people feel scarcity of funds or affluence after looking at others. Such people often say, 'When we were friends in the childhood, we were all equal but now after a lapse of time we do not have such wealth and abundance as our friends.' Such people see only the outer color of life and not look at the inner values and qualities of nature. And consequently, at the time of such comparison, such persons spend an enormous amount of energy of mind and spirit in fighting themselves.

This is the process to defeatism and the one who is the part of this process becomes a defaulter. Always remember that **'Worry is the misuse of our imagination**' and this will lead to our behavior and performance to defect in every field. One must stop wasting valuable energy in this manner and should look at oneself with a joyful heart that you also have some qualities which others do not have.

Good mother and father, lovely and faithful wife, expert brother and sisters, devoted friend circle, secure life system, healthy body and senses, mind filled with positive and creative thoughts, lack of hostility, pious heart filled with love to all and so on and so forth are the progressive and profound affluence to be desired. Every result also has some hidden causes. Try to observe it. Comparison either puts one in inferiority or superiority complex. Both types of these complexes interfere with personal progress. Think of yourself as a new person every time you have a new source of thinking past has passed away and nothing is constant in this world. Everything and everyone change its form from one to another. So always try to see the new form, new ideas, new values. Thinking attached to past problems holds you back with the thinking that was the very cause of failure. So never waste time by remembering anything good or bad and one should use memorable moments to uplift one's positive experiences.

If you want to achieve your goals and fulfill your ambitions, banish negative thoughts. A simple way to conquer our problems and limitations is to develop an attitude of self-esteem, start the process by this.

MY SOUL (POEM)

'I like my soul, I know my soul,
I see my soul, I love my soul,
No one is mine, mine is none,
No one is God, God is my soul,
So I like my soul…
Mind is full of wrong thoughts,
Desires are like fire for loss,
Sensual pleasure not of soul
So I like …
Pains and pleasures lie in things,
These are imaginations mental strings,
The bliss lies in my soul,
So I like …
All of us same, fulfill with flame,
Worldly out looking, matter's frame,
God is hidden in my soul,
So I like my soul.'

Do this every day and at any time whenever you feel uneasy or disturbed. Repeat this as much as possible sitting in a lonely place until you feel the sense of self-bliss and peace.

14

A Way to Achieve Real Happiness and Prosperity

The real happiness and prosperity lie in the act of Devotion. Sometimes we want them by fulfilling our wishes. Sometimes we want them by collecting things. Sometimes we want them by detaching ourselves from materialistic things. Sometimes we want them by either yoga or by pranayama.

But all these methods are not complete until we know the real nature of oneself, outer things, relations, birth, death cause and the world. So first step is to know everything with devotion. If you know anything without devotion and faith, it will be banished in the adverse situation.

So, first know the nature of oneself which is called **AATMA, JIVA (A Substance with full consciousness).** The other name of oneself is **CHAITANYA**. This substance can never be destroyed by any process, nor be generated by any God or Brahma. So we are AATMA and it lives from beginningless time to endless time. Like aatma, other worldly outer matters are also immortal. But they change from one form to other forms like energy. Aatma or Jiva also changes its forms by taking birth individually at different places. After that, the sense of belonging and possession always remains with us. So the conclusion is we are permanent and all other relations, materialistic things are temporary.

If you always want happiness and prosperity in your life, first get true knowledge. Our knowledge is wrong because we always want to keep all materialistic things with us which is not possible. For this, we earn money, build buildings, create new products, want more relations, name, fame etc.

Once upon a time, there were three saints. They were roaming the street for blessings. Their names were money, prestige, and happiness. They entered a house and asked what would you like to choose from three of us. The person asked for money first. Money stopped there for less time. Then they three met again and they entered into another house. The same question arises, householder said I want Prestige. Prestige stopped there. After some time they met again and they entered into another house and the same question arises. The third householder said I need happiness. But all three stopped there. Householder said I need only happiness. Happiness said where there is happiness, money, and prestige come automatically. This is the fact that happiness and prosperity don't belong to materialistic things.

These are mental states. It totally depends on our Attitude. Attitude relies on our thinking process. Divert your thoughts to change your attitude. It is possible by sustaining the practice.

For doing practice, you must have time for yourself. For this, sit up straight without any strain. Concentrate on your breathing. After 4-5 minutes you will feel a subtle body filled with consciousness. Power and Purity are symbolized by OM and ARHAM. Generate power and purity in your body by deep sound of OM ARHAM. This will make you feel that you are completely detached from your relations, business, and other materialistic things. This feeling of oneness should be strong. The warmth of this will strengthen your thinking process and your attitude too. Power and purity of oneself create real peace. Happiness and Prosperity are the by-products of this supreme peace. Peace is our nature and reality. By this process, anyone can attain long time happiness and prosperity of one-self.

Generally, people living in this world think that 'Happiness is fulfilling dreams.' What we desire? What do we want? If we get desired object, we will be satisfied and if we don't, the mind gets unsatisfied. So, lack of satisfaction converts into miserable condition.

With this, it is clear that unhappiness is the state of mind seeking some object. More desires, more the disturbance of mind. This results in unhappiness.

To learn this science of mind Rishi, Muni always remains in the happy state. They want nothing from this outer world. They want their soul, they experience their own knowledge which is related to their soul. When their mind connected with their soul, they attain a state of oneness. When oneness appears, unhappiness disappears.

JAIN AACHARYA says **"NIRDAVANDVA VRITI ADHYATAM"**. Where the mind experiences duality, unhappiness appears. The mind becomes far away from ADHYATAMA (Spirituality). Attributes of our soul present in the state of bliss. **JAIN AACHARYA KUNDKUND** said that-

एदम्मि रदो णिच्चं संतुत्ठो होइ णिच्च मेदम्हि !

एदेण होई तित्तो तो होहिदि उत्तमं सोक्खं !!

"Aedammi Rado Niccham Santutho Hoi Nicch Medamhi,

Aeden Hoi Titto To Hohidi Uttmam Sokkham !!"

If you want supreme bliss, then indulge in yourself, be satisfied with your soul and feel satiated.

Also, the desires of mind are changeable. These desires change with our age, experience, needs, time, family environment, social and political pressure and so on. As the desires change, happiness flies away. As the mind rises up, the pre-happiness has passed. So the state of happiness in mind never remains constant. Constant happiness is only possible if we use our mind as an instrument to merge into our soul.

A soul is associated with our attributes like knowledge, perception, bliss, power, purity etc. So, the source of happiness lies in inner CHAITANYA. This kind of happiness gives real prosperity. The prosperous mind wants nothing. It has so much potency of positivity. Positive mind always sees prosperity around itself. A man of such kind of mind can see the light of stars even in darkness. He feels natural blowing air better than cooler. He thinks we have eyes, ears, legs, hands, and mind to receive all the prosperity of nature. His heart is always green by seeing the greenery of the earth. This is the real meaning of prosperity. So the happiness and prosperity always live together, work together like the eyes of a man.

□

15
A Letter to Youngsters

Dear Children,

Never get disappointed because disappointments give tensions and tensions can drive us away from ourselves and it motivates us to take the extreme step of suicide. Suicide is a heinous crime. It is like digging out a full grown tree. The tree which has already struggled a lot in the process of growing up. In the same manner, you have also struggled a lot.

When the seed was in the soil, it struggled to germinate. The seed turned into a beautiful sapling because of its capabilities. Otherwise, there were many seeds under the soil, some of them died but it faced all the adversities like bacteria, germs, worms etc. and finally turned out to be a winner, a warrior. In the same manner, you were born after a struggle of millions of sperms to fertilize the egg in the womb And only one sperm succeeded, that was the winner, was able to fertilize the egg in the womb and you were born out of that. So you have been a winner since the time of conception!

The struggle did not end there. There was a vast multitude of struggles in a womb of the mother.

But because of your fighting spirit and desire to survive, you were alive there. You got nourishment from the mother and slowly your body parts developed which prepared you for life. As after germination, the plant spreads its roots in the soil for strength, support, and nutrition, so you were not only in the womb of your mother but in her whole body and your thoughts were there in her mind. This is the reason that your mother loves you even more than your father. You became her heart beat. Because she loves you so much that's why she tolerated the pain of giving birth to you. And see the miracle, when you came into the world your mother was blessed with milk in her breast to feed you. It seems the arrangements for your arrival were made in advance. This again proves that you have a strong desire to survive.

When you had fully developed in the womb, you desired to come out. You suffered the pain but you never gave up. And this fighting spirit brought you out and you became a winner!

When you came into the world you were welcomed here by your parents & relatives. Your parents fulfilled all your needs and desires to their best level. Other species do not have wishes but we human beings have.

All your wishes were taken care of by your family without giving any exposure to harsh realities of life and without any mental and physical pain. As the gardener feels relaxed and happy when the small plant turns into a tree. So were your parents when you passed your school. This is again a proof that you are a winner!!

Now the tree grows further and starts bearing flowers and fruits. The roots grow deeper in the ground. It faces rough weather, sun, and storm, hot and cold, hail and fog, everything, which indirectly makes the tree stronger. In the same manner, human beings also face all the adversities of life like ailments, injuries, sufferings, pains etc. You suffered all these and did not budge from your way or path of progress. Nothing could move you except your willpower.

Dear children how can you think of killing the precious life which you have nourished for so long with so much care and love. The killing of self is one of the most heinous crime. This will be a cheating to those who brought you up, loved you, looked after you, took care of you. There are many who have right on your life. How can you cheat them? If a tree is cut down at the time it is about to bear fruits, what will happen? Now when the time has come that you should repay to those who sacrificed their comforts for you. Instead of getting indebted to them, you are going to give them unbearable pain and loss. Think for a while before taking any step, how they celebrated when you were born, how their faces lit up when you put your first foot on the ground to walk, how cheerful they were on your each and every big or small achievement. And Do you know your this one step can drag them into complete darkness, shame and pain? Why do you want to have the taboo of being a loser?

All parents have a dream for their children that they should get a good education and get well settled in their life. Keeping this in mind your parents sent you away from home for better education so that you could fulfill your and your parent's dream and not end your life because you got fewer marks or you could not make up to a good college or university in one or two or more attempts. If you are studying under the pressure of your parents then tell them clearly that you can't become what they want you to be. But if this is your dream, keep patience, don't distract, who knows what the God has in store for you. Keep working with full dedication and determination. I can say it firmly if you have some guts you will definitely succeed and fulfill your dream. At such crucial time, you need to analyze yourself about your potential and action plan. Listen to what your conscience says to you. If you listen to your inner self and follow it diligently no one can stop you from achieving your target. Always keep in mind that you have been a winner since inception and you will be forever. Don't compare yourself to others. You are unique.

Identify/recognize yourself, have faith in yourself, have faith in God and do have faith in your work. Dear children life is a game play it like a game. There is nothing like loss or gain. The game is for entertainment only. Live the life as it is a festival. As we scale up a mountain, it becomes very difficult and tiring to move a step at greater heights. It so happens in the field of education also. We can get good percentage or grade in lower classes but when we go to higher classes, the percentage and grades go down. No player can hit a sixer on all the balls. But he goes for singles or doubles when the ball misses the boundary. Keep on working with same zeal and energy. Give your hundred percent. Don't lose courage and whenever you get a chance to hit a six, means try to get good percent. The other lesson that we learn from games is **"Accept Victory or defeat with the same spirit"**. Keep on self-congratulating and self-motivating in all circumstances. Enjoy the game of life until the end.

One more question is why do you want to become a CA, IAS, MBA or MBBS? Only to earn money and maintain a good standard of life? Dear children, people hardly know about a person's profession. Only his acquaintances know. So if you don't succeed in one profession, you can change it. You can earn money by becoming something else. What is the need for thinking about ending your life?

Suicide does not mean the end of life. After the end of this life, it will restart in the womb of a mother with the same struggle and hardships. But this time it will be worse than the earlier one because you had ended the good life yourself. You will have to face the consequences of your bad deed of suiciding yourself.

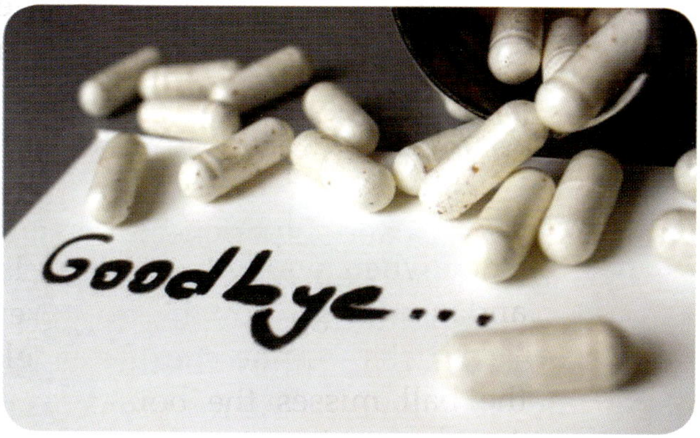

So like a tree maintain your heights. As when it doesn't bear flowers or fruits, at least it provides shade shelter and peace to thousands of birds, insects, and animals. You can become a great source of happiness for your family, friends, relatives and the society at large. Even if you don't become a doctor, engineer, CA or IAS, your presence is the best thing for your family. Your smile is more precious than any treasure of the world for your family. Suppose you get a higher position in life but you are not happy & you are not smiling it is all useless. It is well said **"Achievements are not the way to Happiness; Happiness is the way to Achievements"**. At last, I would like to say don't ever think of ending your life in the company of bad friends. As you would have heard **'A rotten fruit can spoil the whole basket'.**

If we get indulged in one evil, it brings thousands more along with it. So in times of failure don't make friends with evils like smoking, drinking or taking drugs. Sometimes children take to bad habits for entertainment or in the company of friends as a status symbol. These bad habits will attack your self-esteem directly. Keep a distance from these evils and focus on your career. Keep high and pious goals in life. Always follow the right path and if you have problems, face them boldly and leave rest to the wish of the God. You will be a stronger and experienced person after facing problems in life. You will have a treasure of experiences to share with others. Your struggle story can inspire many others in future. In this world you are not the only one who is facing the problems rather there is hardly anyone who has not faced problems. You can find it if you observe it minutely. Don't waste your parents' money and your precious time and life for your friends or bad habits. These bad habits can give momentary pleasure, but they will deceive you of your time, power, wisdom health and money. And after this, there will be nothing left except repentance for the lifetime. Struggles of great personalities like Mahatma Gandhi, Dr. APJ Abdul Kalam, Abraham Lincoln, Edison, Einstein, and others are the great motivational forces which others can follow.

Always keep in mind

Be the change you want to bring in the world.

If you are irritated by every rub, how will you be polished.

Take up an idea, make that one idea your life think of it, dream of it, live on that idea. Let the brain, muscles, nerves, every part of your body be part of that idea and just leave every other idea alone.

Hope is being able to see that there is light despite all of the darkness.

I am a vegetarian and I like all Indian dishes.

Life is the most difficult exam, Many people fail because they try to copy others, not realising that every one has a different paper.

Success is in the other's perspective but bliss and life are in our own.

□

16

Meaning of Independent Living

Nowadays parents face a very awkward situation when their children ask something unexpected or reply in a strange manner. As the children grow and go to school, they want to enjoy a free environment of the college. In college there are no restrictions, boys and girls talk, discuss and study together. They go to any place without restrictions. They want to enjoy the life to the fullest.

But Children think and see around and find how long can you enjoy like this? Do other people in the society live like this? You Feel you are independent. But are you really? Does your life not depend on your parents for monetary help? The status which you are enjoying is due to your parents. If everybody starts wandering freely, what will be future of such a person? Will he become a responsible doctor, engineer, scientist, judge advocate or leader? All the comforts of life like

mobiles or other gadgets have made our life very comfortable. If we spend our time in excessive use of technology, very soon we shall need those people who can save our life i.e. People who are serious towards their life. Excessive freedom means freedom without restrictions and there is a difference between freedom and excessive freedom.

Excessive freedom can make our condition like stray dogs or bulls. A dog gets respect and comfortable life when it is with its master in his house otherwise it is discarded everywhere.

Dear children have a thought whether you want to live a valuable and good quality life or a useless, aimless life. For leading good and quality life, we shall have to behave responsibly. The money and time of your parents and society are spent on you so that you should return the same and do something constructive for the family, society and the nation.

Do you have something constructive for the family, society and the nation? Do you have something to return to the society? If not, then what you are preparing to do in life? If you are not mentally prepared for future responsibilities, you will be an irresponsible person in future, you will be called 'selfish'. Will you like to live with this title?

Student life lays the foundation for future life. Make this foundation strong which will help you get a better career. Be determined to get an honorable position in the society. Eat, play & enjoy but take care of your limits. Try to avoid infatuation in student life. If you are not taking this infatuation in a right way, your future will be spoiled. It can make you a convict and you will have to repent for the lifetime. The attraction for opposite will distract you from your goal and you won't be able to fulfill your dreams and expectation of your parents.

It is a hard fact that we can't focus at two places at the same time. Once you are attracted towards somebody, during your career making time, you won't be able to focus on studies and career and you will lose everything time, money.

Real freedom is that which shows us the path now and we don't have to repeat in future. Real freedom means to think about our self & to be alert. Freedom is an eternal enjoyment, not a momentary joy. The freedom which you think at this stage is sheer madness. When you harm yourself, you harm everybody and you will turn into a bad man/woman. So real freedom means taking complete responsibility. The more responsible you are, the freer you will become.

If you understand the importance of the self, you will definitely be a precious being for all, otherwise, you can cause a great loss to yourself and other.

You would have heard about so many murders in the name of honor killing. Youngsters lose their parents, family and everything for this love affair. This type of affairs leads to divorce soon.

This all brings a bad name to the parents and malign their status in the society. Sometimes, Youngsters are found engaged in multiple affairs which leads to the murder of a lover by other lovers. Such youngster hardly gets any job and live a miserable life.

Blackmailing by boyfriends, gang rape with friends, recording of the videos, change of religion, etc. have become very common nowadays. After taken in confidence, girls are cheated. Many girls have committed suicide to get rid of this shameful situation.

In this selfish world, good people are very less in number. Don't spoil your life for these affairs. Don't be in a hurry to have a relationship. Life is not a movie in which life ends in 3 hours. Real life is totally different. Observe others life minutely. You will know the reality of life.

Dear children progress of life does not depend on independence rather it shines if we are interdependent.

□

17

Awareness is Necessary for Daughters

All the fathers love their daughters very much. They take care of them. They are an apple of their fathers' eyes. Girls can help in getting rid of the bad habits of smoking, drinking, tobacco chewing etc. If she notices that her father is an addict of these evils she should try one or the other method which highlights the harms of these evils. She can show posters, pictures or articles which highlight the effect of these bad habits. She should place such things in different places in the house. Sometimes the father would be annoyed, but don't give up because a father loves his daughter more than these bad habits. It may take time but the effects will be surely positive.

Actor Ram Kapoor, who was a chain smoker and used to smoke 40 cigarettes a day, gave up smoking when his loving daughter asked him a question, **"Papa do you want to die"?** These words had such a deep effect on his head and heart that he gave up smoking forever.

Girls have friends also maybe boys or girls, who can be smokers. They should avoid their company. Don't get indulged in smoking. Dear daughter, I am saying these words because now in India number of female smokers are increasing day by day.

□

18

Respect the Women

Respect for a woman is the respect of the culture of the whole world. The nation, which respects the womanhood, gets the highest respect. Other nations have developed a lot in the spheres of technology but India has a rich cultural heritage. This is the reason that the great personalities like Lord Rama, Krishna, Rishabhdeva etc. were born here. In other countries a woman is not revered so much that's why they don't have any rich cultural heritage. As long as Indians respect the woman as a mother or a sister, India was an ideal for the world to follow. Now there is a decline or change in the point of view of the Indians towards women, that's why our respect at the global level has also declined.

'Love all the women like your mother'- is our cultural belief for the times immemorial and Indians followed it with reverence. This respect for motherhood has been declining for some time in the man. If the reverence for a woman again increases in the hearts of man, it can be said with surety, that the place of woman will go high in the society. The woman will also have to shoulder this responsibility by educating their son or daughter to learn their mother tongue. They will have to inculcate these values in their children. Only then the woman will get back her glorious place in the society.

The child who is educated in mother tongue can respect the mother and the womanhood.

19

Be a Good Listener

You might have heard that we should be a good listener. A woman should listen to her husband & a man should listen to his wife. But while listening, we must also consider the perspective of the speaker. When someone wants to tell you something, you must listen to his/her. This requires a lot of strength. This spontaneous strength can prevent you from an even adverse situation.

Following points should be considered while listening to the speaker:

- If the speaker (husband or wife) is of aggressive nature, then the best option is to keep quiet. But make sure to the speaker that you are listening, only this will make the speaker realize him/her mistake. But not reacting in any way will definitely increase his/her anger.

- If the speaker is not very aggressive, then he/ she will also listen to you carefully. If the speaker doesn't dig out past incidents or divert it to some other direction, then you can try to put your opinion forward.

- If the person is of polite & gentle nature, then you can assure him/her that nothing of this sort will ever happen again. If the speaker replies in negative & say that she/he has heard this from you a lot of times, then you must tell them that you'll be careful from now on & will try to change your habit.

"Anger is a dreadful explosive so it is necessary to avert it from the explosion."

□

20
Power of Mother's Love

When the mother bears her child in her womb she gets attached to it. It becomes the part of her life. The heart beats of the child become the heartbeats of the mother. Even when she falls ill, she thinks about the well-being of the child.

This is a real story which took place in London which proved Medical Science wrong. Holy Cheung Mao Cardics, a 36-year-old Mother, was infected with Virus. Her heart got failed. She was put on the ventilator in Queen Elizabeth Hospital in Birmingham. One day her husband kept her child Jordan near her on the bed. That night her heartbeat was reported normal. The doctors and staff nurses all were very surprised. And now Cheung is all well. As per the reports of the doctors of the hospital she was given 45 heartbeat shocks before it. Later on, she said that I don't know that it is a miracle or not. Three months ago, I felt dizzy while working I went to take doctor's advice. I still remember that doctor asked to take rest but I fell down suddenly.

I was on a stretcher when I got to my senses. I was surrounded by many doctors. I was shocked to hear that I was referred to the Queen Elizabeth Hospital in Birmingham. I was told that I had an attack of Mao Cardics Virus. Slowly and slowly my condition turned bad to worse. Things started appearing hazy. I was craving for my young baby. I was thinking how he would survive without me. How he would drink milk? I had a lot of pain in my heart. At this time I thought of my baby but I couldn't share it with anybody. One day my husband brought my son to the hospital and lay him against me. The feeling, the touch of my child motivated my desire to survive and now I got out of the hospital. (adapted from Dainik Bhaskar, 29 May 2015)

Dear Friends cordial relations have a strong effect. If our relations are good all relatives feel good and when bad all feel bad.

Mother's love is priceless, she is the part and parcel of your life and it gives equal relief to a mother. The anxiety, ambitions, dreams all are connected to the life of her children. Those children who have a strong relationship with their mother will bear the blame of matricide. They are sinners.

□

21

A Wife can Help in Getting Rid of Smoking

Usually when the men come home by driving or when they are moving late hours at the office or they are with their friends, they develop the habit of smoking. Men can get rid of this habit by the love of their wives. Many women have been successful in doing so, you should also try. The best example of this is Barack Obama, who once said, **"I have quit smoking cigarette due to the fear of Michelle".**

You can tell your husband that consumption of tobacco or cigarette can cause various lung diseases like asthma, T.B and can increase the difficulty in breathing. Intelligent people give more importance to their health. If they will regularly consume these things their lifespan will be decreased. A cigarette can reduce 60 to 300 seconds from your life. **"The moment you leave is the moment you improve"**. According to various researchers, the possibility of cancer gets reduced by 16% in first five years. In next 5 years, it's only 8% and in next 30 years, it gets reduced to 2%. That's why you have to make efforts as early as possible. **"Better late than never" and 'The earlier the better'.**

Bollywood actor Amitabh Bachchan has Asthma. When this problem increased the doctor suggested him to leave smoking. Then he determined that he will never think about it again. He left smoking in 1985. It was his firm determination & hectic schedule that kept him away from smoking for so many years. Now, at the age of 75, he works constantly for 10 to 12 hours daily. Moreover, Akshay Kumar, Govinda and Abhishek Bachchan who are renowned cine stars never touch cigarettes.

"Please leave this bad habit.
Because you are the hero of your wife."

□

22

Smoking is Dangerous for All

According to data from 2005 -2010, it has been calculated that the rate of smoking in women has reached up to 25-41%. In this alarming data, Are you also involved? If you are, then make a determination that you will not smoke at all. The result of smoking is very harmful, it decreases the level of estrogen hormone in women's body and sperm count, morphology, and motility in men. Smoking leads to an increase in backbone fracture. Due to this, the bone density decreases and it also leads to miscarriage in pregnant ladies, premature delivery, the birth of a dead child and birth of a mentally or physically handicapped child. Such children have weak immune system and they also face difficulty in development.

Everyone should have to raise their voice against smoking. It is heard that in most of the villages the women's have struggled a lot to ban the liquor shops. Men have an addiction to smoking because they spend most of their time outside their homes, they have work pressure, many types of tensions & most probably bad company.

But now our society is changing fast, there is a lot of change in our society. The women are not just housewives, they have started jobs and services outside. Now the women are contributing equally as men but it is considered to be very horrible for society, tradition, and family.

If our life will be free of smoking, drinking, and all such activities, then only we will become physically and mentally strong and then only the youth of county will succeed. Only successful and progressive youth can create good opportunities for the society.

Former President A.P.J ABDUL KALAM said to children **"Remember that there are two birds sitting on the shoulders of everyone."** On the right shoulder there is an 'ANGEL' and on the left one, there is a 'DEVIL'. When the devil wins people start doing the bad things and when the angel wins the people start doing good things. So how will you make the angel win? Keep in mind when you do the good work, the angel wins and when you do bad things, the devil wins. Because of ignorance, the devil becomes free or independent and by this, he gains strength.

Knowledge makes you the best and successful. People start drinking, smoking and taking drugs because of the influence of the devil. While the influence of an angel will show you the path of truth, non-violence, and humanity.

Once a person told me an incident. This incident took place in Kota where a lot of students (girls and boys) study and live together. A girl used to smoke daily at midnight. Once a policeman saw her. He tried to explain to her but she didn't understand. Then the policeman informed her father about this.

Her father gave a very shocking reply, **"She is my daughter, she is living her life, let her live her life in a way she wants."** If all the parents have the same opinion about the freedom of their children, then we can imagine what do they want.

In such thought society, knowledge and nation will totally degenerate, by the time our youth will indulge in evils, theft, corruption, and terrorism. These all are wrong activities which we can see in today's society.

According to the survey of GATS (Global Adult Tobacco Survey), the number of people who smoke has increased from 25.2% to 41.6% in India. Psychologist says that women smoke and take drugs because of work stress.

Nowadays smoking is a fashion/trend for women. Some feel that Nicotine in cigarette makes their body slim. Some think that it is an energy booster. Some do so to copy their favorite model/actress. Apart from this women should take care that addiction of all these things will harm them more as compared to men because it may lead to an imbalance of hormones released in women's body which can create a serious disease in their body. To get rid of stress, tension and loneliness a person should eat some fruits, take fresh juice and do exercise in the morning and in the evening. Reading motivational books will definitely provide benefit. Also, they should keep themselves busy in their work.

This is my suggestion to all. It is not a rule or law because wise people only need a suggestion, which is more than enough.

□

23

Time Tested Tips for Success

No one can live alone whether it is a homely man or a saint. Everyone needs to live in a group and it is very difficult for two fellows to live together without any clashes. If this clash is related to each other's nature or for the improvement, then it is never going to end with differences of ideology no one can change the nature of others. There are only two ways to change somebody:- First is **"The one who wants to change his nature, should feel about the need of the change"** and the second is **"The person who wants to change some body's nature, should be very wise, peaceful and serious."**

This situation of bringing changes can be between husband & wife, brother & sister, brother & brother, father & son, teacher & pupil, colleagues or any other relations.

From the above-mentioned methods if we discuss the first one then it is very difficult to make the concerned person realize about his negative, pessimistic nature. For this, we can ask the person to read the books which highlight this type of nature. If it is possible, it is very good if not, then try at the second one. The person, who wants to bring changes in others, should be very tolerant and peaceful. The person who is temperamental/aggressive and abusive should not try this.

There is a short incidence related to this. A saint had many followers/pupils. All were very worried because of one pupil as he was a thief. Once when he was caught, people complained to their Guru. The Guru did not react. After a few days, he stole again. Other pupils complained to the Guru again. The Guru assured them that everything will be alright gradually. This was repeated many times and finally, all the pupils reached before the Guru and requested him to punish him otherwise they all will go away from there. There were two groups before the Guru. On one side the thief and the other side the other pupils. The Guru addressed the group of pupils, **"You all are very wise. You understand the difference between good and bad, sin and virtue. You keep yourself away from the evils. You have really learned my teachings."**

But this pupil has not yet learned the difference between good and bad. So how can I leave him? You can leave if you want to. But I cannot let him go. After hearing the words of his Guru, the thief was in tears. He realized how his Guru was ready to leave all his pupils for his sake. He fell in his guru's feet and promised that he would never steal again. After that, he never did any stealing. This short account is sufficient to guide those who want to change others.

Most often the reformers want to suppress others by getting aggressive. They feel that their threat or scoldings will improve the person. This method will never bring improvement rather it will affect mutual affection between them. The Great Acharyas have rightly said, **"Krodhat Preetivinashah" means anger kills affection.** How deep the affection may be, it will be ruined by the first attack of anger and its continuous use uproots the love & affection very soon. The aggressive person considers himself very powerful but in actual he is very weak from inside. He is not able to control his weakness so he expresses it through his anger. The aggressive person is found to be egoistic. Whenever his ego is hurt, he loses control over his temper. Some people are aggressive by nature and at the same time they may be religious as well they may be having good self-control.

A dictator is devoid of self-confidence. He can do the act of bravery but by crossing the limits. He does such work very easily for

which a tolerant man may feel hesitant.

Alexander, the great, was terrorized by his own dictatorship. He did not have faith in anyone and always thought that nobody belonged to him. Because of lack of faith, he was killed in his party by his own people. This is the fate of a dictator. It is rightly said:

"Quiet and Cool Temperament is the most important quality of a person who is destined to rule".

□

24
Arrogance of Mind

The mind is arrogant like a spoilt child. Once the child is spoiled, it becomes very difficult to manage him. It is wise to take care of the child before he gets spoilt. Keep on telling him that he can improve one day. It can be the threat of parents which keeps him away from the sins and bad company. The same situation is there with the mind. Learn to counsel your mind. Try to preach yourself. The mind which works wisely of sometimes gets sad at spoiling of the things and gets cautious for future. It's not necessary that the mind will change its habit of getting punishment. When the mind is nurtured with knowledge of values (Sanskars), it destroys lust.

Aacharya Pujya Paad has rightly said that **"The punished mind is just like an obstinate criminal which gets indulged in criminal activities again and again after completing the punishment."** Sometimes he is not in a position to decide for his life whether he should improve his habit or counsel his mind. A wise man is always conscious of committing sins. The Greatest saint's mind also gets indulged in crime. By his enlightenment, he gets conscious about his smallest and minutest sins and tries to save his mind from that.

Lust does not die in the enlightened state and even after a lot of self-control. It can be improved again & again by practice. That's why in Jainism giving pain to body and mind are external austerity. It may or may not benefit the soul. Self-study and meditation are called internal austerity. Self-study makes us guilty, conscious and meditation removes the root cause of the sin.

The one who feels that he is a real Saadhak, Yogi or Seeker, his eyes which were very excited to see the beauty, now get closed down at the same sight. This reflects the controlled mind of a person who has got a hold of all the desires. If the eyes try to satiate by seeing the beautiful things, the Saadhak or Yogi understands this and protest against it. After practice, the mind gets so unwilling that the person would not even raise his eyes on things and he becomes a real 'Saadhak' or 'Yogi'. So keep on improving your mind. Counsel it, scold it, punish it, again and again before it turns into a spoilt child.

□

25
Quest for Knowledge

All the living beings have the appetite for food whether animals or human beings. But the appetite for knowledge is found in human beings only. Indulgence in entertainment & yoga has always flourished together. Those who have a quest for knowledge get inclined to Yoga. It seems that the today's man's quest for knowledge has died, that's why philosophers and sages are not commonly seen. All are moving around money and fame. The one who cannot give new dimensions to his knowledge is like a dead animal. The one who has the desire to gain knowledge feels fresh every day. Knowledge is the treasure of soul which differentiates between a man and an animal. The one, who thinks about himself and for his soul, becomes a Samyak i.e. the one who has a feeling of equality for all.

On the contrary, getting knowledge for worldly pleasure leads to degeneration of the soul and the soul does not expand to other living beings for their help. If we focus on ourselves, the mind can see all the movements wisely. That's why a Yogi is

always of peaceful temperament and he always remains cheerful. Nothing is new in this world. If we easily accept changes and the expansion of soul, we shall never be sad. The absence of sadness & sorrows newness. This newness will not be there by doing something but it will be there when they're to a halt in doing something. When we do something we are worried about loss or gain. It needs efforts, hard work to do something and the happiness of gratification of desires means stability of seeing and knowing. It also means ending of worries and desires. If you want to do something for the outer world, minimize the expansion of 'I', i.e. your ego. If you want to do something new for others, try to fulfill your needs from your surroundings. If you want to do something new, don't desire to amass wealth. If you want to do something new, keep yourself in the company of gnostics. If you want to do something new, help the helpless. If you want to do something new from inside, forgive everyone. If you want to do something new from inside, be friendly with everybody. If you want to do something new internally, keep yourself away from the divine power and miracles. If you want to do something new internally, control your mind. If you want to do something internally, convert your attachment into detachment. If you want to do something externally, have motherly or sisterly feelings for every woman. This change from inside is the change of nature. But to fulfill all these dimensions, the most important thing is a quest for knowledge.

Knowledge makes us capable. But there is a need for one more thing which makes knowledge capable and not the knowledgeable person. It is very necessary to take care of the knowledge. And to express knowledge and to use it properly we need the strength of self. Where there is the strength of self, there is tolerance. If there is a power of self, there is tolerance. Somebody has said, **"A capable person lacks tolerance."** If there is patience with knowledge, no one can harm that knowledge. Most people take themselves capable of the style of their thinking, expression and the way of impressing before others. This is the biggest mistake of life. Actually, wisdom comes with patience and **"Kshyopsham Karma." (The Karmas whose some qualities are covered and others are uncovered are called Kshyopsham)**. The Karma of **'Viryantraay'** i.e. strength is equally important. There should be a balance between **'Kshyopsham Karma'** and **'Viryantraay.'** Sometimes there is not a balance between these two. That's why sometimes educated people to get mad, sad and get into depression. Aggressiveness with wisdom indicates lack of strength and patience.

□

26

Love - An Essential Part of Life

Everyone wants love in life and they like it. Love makes the person feel complete. If we want to start loving, we will have to connect with others. Connecting with others is the beginning as well as the end of love. The reason is, if we want to do something by depending on others, the end is inevitable. A need of others means dependence on others. Dependence on others leads to clashes, clashes lead to fear, anxiety and finally, self-defeat. Every soul wants to love the nature and mix-up with the creation of the God. This can be possible only when the man is free from all types of desires and is away from expectations. Loving the self-means living within oneself, living up to oneself and connecting to self. After reaching up to self if the man accepts himself and agrees that he has connected to self and we are connected to him. When you will get so complete in yourself that you won't realize that others are connected to you. At the same time, you won't have your desires. This is the right path to become complete. This is also the right method to be free from clashes, fearless and self-dependent.

We should have a relationship of love with those who have gone through this path. Our love with Arihant and pure noble souls never make us dependent, rather make us independent. If we want to be complete, we should have relations with such complete personalities. The indifference of such complete personalities never makes us sad as we want to become the same. This knowledge aggravates desire and this desire is known as devotion, love, dedication. Even after becoming a slave of such personalities we do not feel as if we are their slaves. We feel free even after getting dependent on them.

The personality which is imperfect is incomplete in himself. It may be possible that he would be moving on the path of getting complete. Connecting to such an incomplete person will make him feel dependent on others and will create obstacles in the path of that person. If the union of the incomplete man is in coordination, it can give us speed. If an incomplete man sits in a crowd or collects the people or tries to regulate it and by doing so, he thinks he is complete, he will surely get distracted and this attachment will be a hurdle for him. He may overestimate his power on seeing the crowd and the affection around himself, this is surely a deviation from the aim/goal. The way to be complete is very tough. It can be very easy if your mind is not overpowered by attachment or greed.

This is a fact that the complete person will be visible even if he is not in front of the eyes. We should have faith in them. You will find an incomplete man on the way. We will have to use such a spectacle which can help you see the things which are closer as well as which are far away. As both sights are properly fixed in the spectacles, in the same manner, we will have such a balance in our thoughts. While using such spectacles we can see both in the same manner. Farsightedness will move us on the path of progress and nearsightedness will tell us the record of our success. There should be a speed in progress and progress in speed. Speed and progress should go hand in hand without disturbance. The combination of these two is the bliss forever. It will give self-confidence and the pleasure of independence.

We will have to show dedication towards the incomplete man only then we will become complete. You may feel that the person, for whom you are showing dedication, does not take you according to your wish. You may have numerous expectations from such a person, but remember that many other persons would also be dedicated to him whose expectations he has to take care. Overall we should not keep negative feelings for such a person. If our devotion is real, then we should try to change yourself not him. Whatever he gives, we should use it for our well being. We should not think how much and what he is giving to others. If we do so our dedication will be real.

Once there was a kind-hearted, generous, people loving king. All his servants were very loyal, as the king loved them like his own children. It was his nature to be sad in their sadness and happy in their happiness. There was one more servant whom he loved especially. One day, the king was going on a safari with him. The king saw that there was a tree bearing only one fruit. The king picked up the fruit and gave a piece of it to the servant. He said that it was very delicious and demanded one more piece. The king gave him, he again demanded, the king gave him again. Finally, only a small piece was left, the king thought that he should also taste the fruit which is so tasty. So he ate the last piece. It was so bitter that the king spits it over there and asked his servant reason for eating the fruit. **The servant replied, "The hands which have given me so delicious fruits if one out of them is bitter, I should not make complaints."**

This example teaches us that we should always remember past generosity & kindness. Don't be thankless if one thing is not according to your wish. We should have dedication and courage to bear the bitter experiences calmly. This bitter experience will take you on the path of success. Your devotion will get deeper. A person with the weak mind will show devotion & dedication very soon. But if there is lack of courage with dedication & lack of stability of mind, the relation will not last any longer. The relation becomes deep and firm only when we learn something from our present incidence and try to be tolerant. Take happiness and sadness with the same spirit, you will be able to save yourself from the pain of sadness. You will enjoy both of these equally.

From this example, we need to learn that we should accept bitter things in a graceful manner. Our reluctance should not reach our reverend Guru. We should be simple as a child, as the child forgets his mother's slap as quickly as he gets a toy from her. Even if we don't get any toy we need to be quiet. So drink the bitter drink from your reverend Guru calmly. If others get to know, you will feel insulted. If you want to live a good life, always be happy and don't take bitter words seriously.

No one is born without problems in life. Problems will be always a part of life. As we can cure any illness by its correct diagnosis, so we have to take the problem as an illness. We have to find out the root cause of the disease. Is it possible to cure it? How long will it take? What is the tonic for this? If we think about the above mention questions, we can find the solution to this problem very easily. Problem is not a 'thing', it is a series of thoughts only like 'it may not cause some evil to us', 'it may not cause some loss', 'we may not be insulted', 'they may not hate us' etc. etc. Many times we feel there is a big problem, though the matter is trivial. Many times there is no reason for jealousy and hatred. Sometimes a small doubt or confusion becomes the cause of differences in relationships. We need to observe the facts. As long as we do not observe the things minutely, we can't find its correct solution. More than half of the problem is solved if we do the self-analysis of its causes.

Sometimes we have high expectations from somebody and when he is not able to reach up to our expectations, we feel we are cheated and it becomes the cause of differences. Personal problems can be solved at the personal level. Mostly our doubtful nature is the root cause of this. We need to spare some time for self-observation and when we feel this feature in our nature, we should try to change it. No one can change us as long as we don't have a strong determination for it. No one can end our problems as our problems are only because of us. Blaming others for this is just useless.

Sometimes the problem can be of a group. Members of the group may oppose you. You may not find anyone in your favor, everybody would have doubt on you. You can solve such a difficult problem by changing your nature. Try to analyze which of your action is the cause of differences in the relationships and reason of your insult. Why does this happen again and again? You will find the reasons, if you do not follow them, your life will run smoothly. This can be possible only if we want to improve. In group problem also we can improve the things by changing our behavior, thoughts, and cheerful nature. When we change our perspective or mind our doubts will be removed and it will convert to the faith. So keep your attitude positive. Make people sure that you are not irritated because of them. Face them with smiling face. Even after being disturbed if you face them as if nothing has happened, this habit will change their perspective towards you. Even if you are only doing drama, but from inside you are unhappy and worried, don't show any glimpse of this and if you succeed in doing so, most of your problems will disappear. This will do something good today and just now. Don't think of distant future.

The chain of thoughts related to future problems can last for very long. We have to stop this thought process because this is called worry. Have a belief that what you are thinking is never going to happen. Sometimes we get so worried and frightened due to our negative thoughts which affect our health, make us mentally disturbed. It is well said, **"I've had a lot of worries in my life, most of which never happened."** We should not praise or criticize anyone. We should not get satisfied or annoyed with somebody very quickly. If we have such a fickle mind then we are surely going to be in tension not only for today or tomorrow but for the lifetime. Our attachment, friendship or relationship with anybody should be independent and not disturbing.

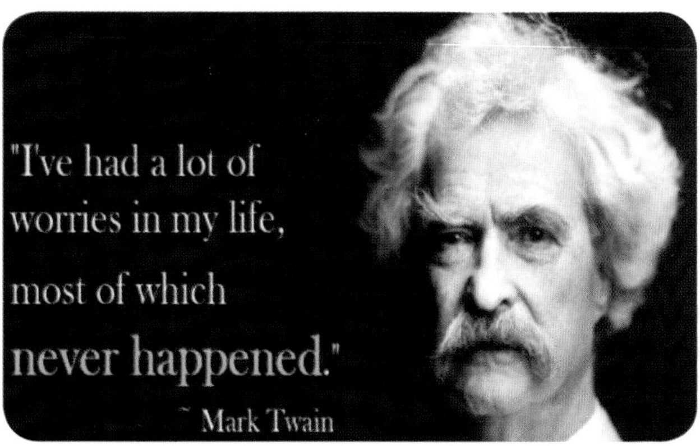

Showing our right to others can spoil our relationship. Don't be so close to anybody that you become a hurdle in his progress. There should be a good understanding of each relationship which will not make you dependent on others or others should not be dependent on you. Most often we want that others should depend on us, they should need us. This thought makes us egoistic which can't be satisfied and leads to anger which spoils love. Aacharya Bhagvanta's have understood this secret that's why they have written **"Krodhaat Preetivinashah"** i.e. Anger Kills Love. So have forgiveness and equality. Those whose mind is not in the balanced state gets satisfied or angry very quickly. Such nature becomes the cause of worries for himself and for his close relatives. It is said

"Kshane rushta Kshane tusht, Rushtstusht kshane-kshane. Avyavasthit Chintanam, Prasadoapi bhayankar."

Means those who get happy and annoyed quickly, the favor of such people who have disturbed mind is also terrible. People with such nature often remember the goodness or kindness they show to you. And if you don't reciprocate in the manner, they will tell it to you for a long time and will get annoyed with you. Later on when you try to persuade them only then they will open their heart. Such type of mood is called negative melancholy. Such people are non-enthusiastic, annoyed, tempered and critics. Kindness or generosity shown by such people is a burden which they always carry on their heart and when the person receiving these gets to know this he also feels burdened.

Don't be afraid of this behavioral problem. Make effective efforts.

Lord Mahavira has rightly said, **'Parasparopagraho Jivanam'** means showing interdependence on each other is the religion of all the living beings. Show kindness to all, this is enough. Interdependence is religion, which means happiness. In this state, the person does not have the feeling of revenge that's why this type of kindness is called self-kindness.

When kindness shown on others is affected by ego, it becomes a selfish act, and anyone who has shown this type of kindness will surely express it to others. This is called weakness of mind.

Such people think that they are idealistic. Such people announce others against the rule if the work is not done according to their wish. Such people can impress others by their words but actually, they are far away from their words. They even don't hesitate to use wrong words. By expressing ourselves with bad or wrong words we create the situation like vomiting and spoiling the place. A tolerant person can only digest such words. Winston Churchill, the PM of Britain has rightly said, **"Digesting ill words without speaking has not spoiled anybody's digestive system"**. Selection of correct words shows positivity and creativity of the person. Short positive thoughts can inspire somebody. We can do so only when we have positive thoughts. If we pretend to be positive but do not follow the same in our life we can't leave a permanent impression on others.

There were two boys stuck up in stormy weather. The first child's mother shouted, **"Get hold of the branch firmly or you will fall down".** And the second child's mother said calmly, **"Dear child get hold of the branch firmly so that you may not fall"**. The first child could not tolerate the stormy wind and fell down but the second one got hold of the tree for 45 minutes and was safe. Actually, the words of their mothers had a great impact on the psychology of the boys. The first child heard the negative words of his mother and fell down and the second one got strength from the positive words of his mother and could hold firmly for so long.

□

27

Why do We Get Worried?

I think the man himself is responsible for his worries. If he thinks that he would not get worried, no force of this world can make him worried. If there is nobody to help, then there can be some problems. Many people think that others should come and help. You can help such people wholeheartedly, give time but they still remain unsatisfied as long as they don't see the anxiety on your face. If you help them calmly they won't praise you. On the contrary, they make friends with those who cry and get nervous soon. Later on, they praise them a lot. This reflects that a worried and anxious person feels satisfied to see somebody in the same situation.

Feeling of competition with others can be one of the reasons for worries. This feeling of competition arises from jealousy. Mostly this feeling can be observed among persons living together. These seeds of jealousy germinate when the person finds his friend in trouble and he feels happy. When somebody finds fault in your friend and tells you at that time the roots of jealousy grow faster. Everyone wants to have new relationships. If the new fellow likes him, he feels good, but when the new fellow is very cunning, shrewd and breaches the trust, then the condition becomes critical. For a devotee, there should not be any feeling of competition. Ambition is the mother of competition. Amidst such feelings, we can work by focusing on some good aim. There should be no feeling of competition as it can lead to jealousy. We should learn from those who are ahead of us. It's not necessary that we will work with them. A good devotee follows on his own path. If our soul is invisible, then the way to reach the soul should also be invisible. Some devotees are very extrovert. Those devotees who are not so extrovert or new devotees or old devotees who are not able to create external impact should not get distracted. Our past, as well as our present Karmas, are the bases of our permanent or long-term achievements. We can't create any effect only because of present Karmas. Still, pious Gurus and 'Manishees' with their talent and personality, have contributed to the greater social causes. They have devoted wholeheartedly to their action, speech, and thoughts.

Here I'm talking about the welfare of the larger society. Sometimes a devotee of lower caliber or a beginner gets highly influenced by the fan following of other great devotees and does the same blindly and thoughtlessly which results in difficulties and pains in achieving that aim. So I would like to say that our thought, action, and body should not get involved in the rat race of accomplishing our ambitions rather it should be for fulfilling larger social aims. When the aims are high, they don't create obstacles in works of welfare but when they are narrow, they reflect egotism and selfish motives, which can never do anything for welfare. Such works may fulfill your aim but they will never be for the upliftment of the society and the self. In the same manner, we can differentiate a great personality and a common man. We can say **"Great minds have purposes but others have wishes".** This means that great people have the objectives and others have wished.

□

28

Make the Best Use of Your Talent

Sometimes people misuse their talent. There are some qualities or talents that can be learned with very little efforts and we get a lot of appreciation and it fills our life with happiness and prosperity but they are very temporary and affect other qualities or talents. This talent is the talkative nature.

Talking to everyone, cracking jokes, telling stories are some habits which give us temporary happiness but deviate us from our other talents and we feel looted. Some people don't waste their energy in temporary pleasure but they invest for the improvement of their permanent talent. Such people win the credit of successful personalities in life. Though it may take a long time this credit or honor gives more self-satisfaction, acknowledgment, and praise.

It is correct that temporary satisfaction and happiness are not real. They are a drunkard who feels happy and forgets their pain after drinking. But when he comes to senses he is more tensed, unhappy and disturbed for wasting his time and money and going on a wrong track. Fun & Frolic can give us joy but that is like a soap bubble, short-lived. Mostly we try to overlook the problem or do not have the courage to solve it. Most often we forget that there is a solution to every problem. If there is a lock, surely there will be its key also. Every question has an answer. Similarly, God doesn't give any problem without its solution. So never worry, efforts always succeed.

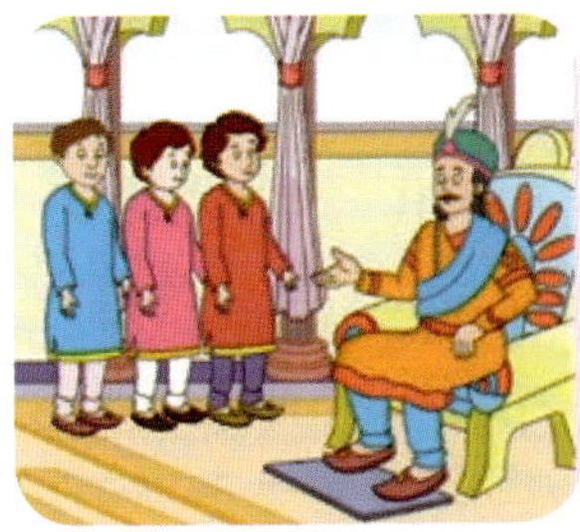

Here is a story of a king who had ordered to hang three persons, but still he wanted to give one chance to each. The three persons were locked in three separate rooms and told who so ever comes out of the room, his punishment will be forgiven. All the rooms had only one door and guard locked and left away from there. The first person thought that the king was joking, he will hang us and he can't do anything. The second one walked around the room but could not find any solution. The third one woke up in the morning and observed that the door was closed and thought that it would be locked from outside. He still shook the door and knocked it. The door opened and he came out. The guard had just closed the door and slightly bolted it which could be opened by shaking. The persons inside thought that the doors were locked. The third person worked in the right direction and got success and was finally able to save his life.

Once upon a time, a king asked the last wishes of two persons who were given punishment of hanging. The first person did not say anything but the second one said he wanted to teach his highness's horse how to fly. He wanted to take time of a year. The king said he would announce his decision the next day. Both the persons were together at night. The first one blamed the second one that he wanted to escape by telling lie. The second person said that it was not a matter of right or wrong but it is to pass the time. He further said that it is sure that he would be killed but in this one year there can be four possibilities. The first can be that the king may die within a year. The second is that I can die. The third is that the horse may die and the fourth one is that the horse can learn how to fly.

This story may be unreal and full of imagination but it is good to show the right path to the wise persons indirectly. Knowledge with wisdom is a great strength. But in today's world, it is ironical to know that the man is with **"More degree but less common sense"**. Earlier I did not take such stories seriously. As these all are unrealistic. I took them of no use. But now I think earlier life was like walking on a straight road without any twists or turns, ditches or bumps, obstacles or rocks. At that time I preferred bigger issues but now these small incidences impress me a lot. I value them.

It seems that after walking on a straight road now the turn has come to scale a mountain. Now while moving up, I have understood the value of each and every breath and step, and the need to put each step cautiously. That's why I have started liking minor issues. At such times we need to remember the kindness of our Gurus. This remembrance gives me positive energy in an adverse situation and teaches me not to lose courage rather keep patience and be honest.

On my lonely journey, his presence in the heart is a great support and it boosts up my self-confidence.

Once a man saw a dream that he was walking along the beach. He noticed that there were two pairs of step, and thought that the God was with him. Then he saw that he was in an adverse situation and there was only one pair of footsteps on the soil. He became very sad thinking that the God also left him alone in adversities of life. But he felt as if the God had answered. The God said that he was always with him because of his dedication, his firm faith. The one pair of steps that you are seeing here is mine because I lifted you in my lap at that time. When we remember generosity and kindness of others it develops the feeling of thankfulness. This is one of the precious quality but it is essential for the development of the personality. All the relations may be of Teacher-Pupil, Leader and Public, Father and son are nurtured by this feeling of thankfulness.

When thankfulness and diligence or dedication come together in a person, it helps in overall development of the person. Dedication motivates us to do our work continuously. A dedicated person does not have any monastery. The work of the diligent person is a great lesson for the society. Whether it is a religious guru or a politician, diligence brings the qualities of leadership. The work which is without any show-off or greed and without attachment can be for the upliftment of the society or nation. The leader who works with the feeling of indifference is called a Yogi. Such a dedicated Yogi is a real Champion of the nation.

The Digambar saint who wanders everywhere and without worldly pleasures and is indifferent to materialistic greed is an eternal source of spiritual energy. In addition to this are Grihasth Yogis, who serve the nation from the highest posts. Such yogis work for the welfare of the masses. In the absence of such Yogis, the nation is not progressing ahead even after scientific developments. Progress is a show-off but the downfall is a loss which cannot be compensated even after centuries. When we hear about the tremendous progress of our country and that many Indians are among the richest millionaires, we feel that our people are progressing. It brings a lot of pride to the nation. On the other hand, we also hear the number of the poorest of the poor is also increasing. It hurts a lot. This type of progress is like a tree which is laden with flowers and fruits but its roots are not given nutrients and also they are not protected from insects which are eating up the roots. Growth should be like **'Vat Vriksh' - Banyan Tree**. It grows externally and internally at the same speed. But this type of development is missing in case of the nation. External progress is visible but the growth of spiritual and basic needs are missing.

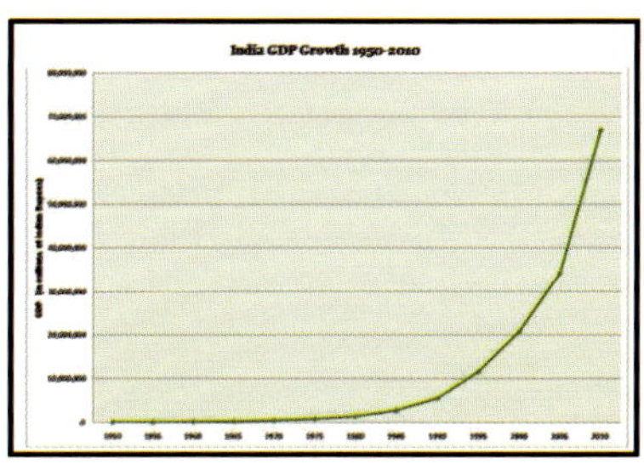

This is the reason why we are frightened to even after development. We are drifting away from the basic realities. This can be estimated by the example that after Independence from 1950 to 2009 the GDP has risen from 0.4% to 39.1% in these 60 years. But still, there are 40% Indians who are poor. According to some facts, 70% people earn only Rs.50 per day. The reason for this is the irregular distribution of money among the people. There is no deficit of money but the reason is that it is not reaching up to all the sections of society. They are not getting the profits of the plans which are introduced for them. It is just like the energy in our body, if it is not supplied to all the organs properly, we will fall ill and if it prolongs it can be fatal. That's why political or religious leader can work without taking care of the needs of all. This problem has become quite common in politics, diligence is declining day by day. In the religious field also our religious Gurus are getting spiritually bankrupt and they are busy in increasing their followers by cheap popularity. Outer show off and desire for popularity have deviated them from their basic work. They are using more power of the senses than their spiritual energy. They are busy in fulfilling their desires. They are far away from spiritual and mental peace. Such fraud saints keep on preaching about happiness and peace. Diligence means self-less service and character. According to Newton,

"A man of good character becomes a great man and nobody else".

□

29
Tips to Excel in Life

There are many people who are always worried about doing something. They want to Excel. They want to be the best. They think that they have wealth, wisdom & strength and they can do whatever they want to. They feel proud of their past achievements. But still, they can't become great. Let's try to understand this with the help of a short story by Yuki Elkin who is an author in Russian & English language.

There was a man in a village. He wanted to achieve all those things which he could get. He was overwhelmed with this thought. He had only one dream that he wanted to show his excellence in all the fields. There were many areas where he could work and he could rule over the world provided that he focused on them. He knew there were boundless possibilities like he could write books, he could do some inventions, or he could accumulate power to uplift the lives of millions. He used to live with a power in himself. He had only one hurdle and that was that he had only one life i.e. limited time. He had to decide where he could focus his boundless capabilities. It was really a tough task because selecting one means keeping away the rest of the options. Meanwhile, he completed his education, got a job and then married and had his children and started taking care of all these. But whenever he was free, he used to think about using all his power to get an exceptionally excellent life.

He got success in the works he took in his hands. He got a lot of respect from people. During this also he kept on consoling himself of doing something excellent in the field of his choice. The time passed, he got old. Meanwhile, some doors of opportunities had already closed. Day to day work, responsibilities of children and family, problems of daily life kept him busy and one day he had pain in his chest. He looked himself into the mirror and noticed that he had got old, his hair was grey and eyes were looking tired. He was devoid of any energy and enthusiasm. And the next moment his breathing stopped and he left this world. The message of Yuki's story is that the excellence was just one step ahead. He could do a lot but he wasted his life.

Dr. Terry Orlick, the author of book **"Pursuit of Excellence" says that "We don't need two**

or three lives for getting excellence. But it is very easy. Actually, everyone wants to live an excellent life and the situations do not make any difference. Conditions to be a better human being, capabilities to accumulate wealth, good health, and struggle for betterment are a few ways which can make our life exemplary."

Excellence is achieved by regular efforts. Those who sleep in the early mornings they are found lazy throughout the day. We should get up before or at the time of sunrise. If we wake up early, when there is still some darkness, we can have the glimpse of the divine power inside us. At this time we have the storage of energy that we need for the whole day. Good thoughts also arise in our mind at this time.

□

30

The Ideology of Anekaantik Dharma

For gaining the maturity of thoughts and tolerance Jinendra Bhagwants adopted Syaadwaad method and expressed their thinking by Anekaant Dharma. Earlier Anekaantwaad and Syaadwaad were the means of spreading a religion. But today we need these methods to consolidate our thoughts on tolerance, tolerating other's progress, taking other's equivalent to yourself, not having expectations from others and keeping a hold on our own expectations. Expectations should be according to time. Parents expectations from the child should be according to his age. It's not necessary that the son who was doing something before marriage would be able to meet the same expectations after the marriage. As the age grows so are the responsibilities. In such a situation one single 'Mantra' like thinking i.e. narrow-mindedness can disturb the peace & harmony of the whole family. There is boundation in self-control but one can have self-control after being free from attachments. One can manage the relations and maintain love and affection in them in **'Nirbandh'** (i.e. free from attachment) state also.

A man had a tame parrot. They loved each other very much. Once the parrot flew away on finding the cage open. The man was grieved to know this and thought that not only human beings but animals also cheat. He was in sorrow of love. One day he was returning from a village. The journey was long. So to relax, he decided to sit under a tree. He was quite sad. The parrot came over and got seated on his shoulder. It started talking to them lovingly. The man became very happy. As he had to reach back to his town, so he started his journey. The parrot brought fruits for him, which satiated his hunger. The man praised the parrot very much. And after some time, the parrot flew away. There is a message in this story that you can love somebody in Nirbandh state also i.e. without boundations. It is not necessary to be in boundations we can say.

The relation is like a bird,
If you hold it tightly it dies,
If you hold it loosely it flies,
Hold it affectionately.... so that
It remains with you forever.

We should try to understand the needs of others along with our greed and mental satisfaction. It's not necessary that a person can always live with you. Parents should not have same expectations from their children after their marriage. They should think that the son/daughter has to spend a long life with his/her spouse. Keeping this in mind we should give them the freedom to spend time and understand each other. If the parents are not doing this then they are responsible for the marital problems of their children for the lifetime.

Marital problems are very common in the youth. Estrangement in relations & divorce is increasing day by day. These problems can arise due to the shortage of time. When one of them focuses more on the career than the relationship or it may be because of nature. So everyone, who wants to be a successful person in all spheres of life, should change himself with time. This should be followed in all relations like between two friends, students, master & servant, teacher & pupil.

The relations, which are for the gratification of the ego, will never get successful. We should not use any relationship for our personal gains. If so happens, the relations get extremely bitter, the person concerned can revolt and lead to separation. The man is worried in the absence of Syaadwaad and Anekaantik philosophy.

The man is entangled in the web of relations like father, son, uncle and friends and so on. Along with it, there are some professional relations also. The man has forgotten the real cause of these diverse relations. The cause is to know nothing about the soul. **"Anekmekam cha Padsya Vachyam"** means one word has different forms and meanings.

The same happens to our soul. Soul has so many relations with the body with different perspectives. Realize that in all relations our soul is one. From the perspective of our son, we are a father, with the perspective of our father we are a son and so on. This is called Anekant. So many forms in one soul or in any matter always lie.

Among all these, the one, who forgets the soul, can never get out of problems. If you don't have faith in the soul, means you don't have self-confidence. Nowadays people have made the meaning of self-confidence very shallow. People take the determination of doing any work and completing it strictly as self-confidence. But actually, when the faith of our conscience produces the strength, that strength is called self-confidence. A Common man sometimes takes himself as a king, slave, queen, inferior, superior and so on. Sometimes he feels defeated, at the other time as a champion. Sometimes he considers himself the wisest and the other moment as the foolish one. But the most precious is our soul. The basis of the tree is its seed. Still, we water the leaves and flowers. The tree does not grow by watering the leaves.

A confident person should be calm. A Calm person is very cool. These can play an important role in the qualitative improvement. It helps in character formation and personality development. A confident person is self-centered also he can help in the social and national development. In this process, there are two prominent enemies - lust and anger. Ravana was overpowered by lust and was the reason for the creation of the Ramayana. On the other hand, Duryodhana was overpowered by his anger and Mahabharata was written after him.

The proportion, in which these two evils keep on increasing in the soul, will make the path to destruction easy. Letting these two evils not to grow in the mind is called self-control. Without controlling these evils and following the conscience, it is not easy to rule the state whether he is a king or king of kings. Anger can be expressed by body, mind, and thoughts, but by controlling the words, you can control the anger. Mostly in anger, we start abusing others which makes the listener angry. The best remedy to control anger is to keep quiet. There is a posture recommended for keeping quiet. Keep your tongue stick to the palate and sit in Gyan mudra i.e. by joining thumb and first finger. Leaving that place can be another option. Make a resolution that **"I will always speak without getting angry. In the worst situations also, I would not use abusive language and would not show uncivilized behavior."** If you succeed in doing so, you will be the happiest, peaceful and the most beautiful person in the world.

There can be different methods for this. Once a sage prepared a medicine for anger and told the people that when they are angry they had to put it in the mouth, but they would not drink it. People did the same. It was very effective. When people asked about it, he told that it was nothing but water. Actually, it was used to stop the person from speaking at the time he was in anger, which automatically reduced the quarrels. You can have some water in your mouth also. If there is no water then you can inhale some air in mouth and keep it intact for some time.

Scientists have suggested that we can eat some sugar when we get angry. These all methods are for diverting the mind for some time. It is well said that **"Silence is man's best friend in the agitated state."**

An angry person first hurts himself then speaks badly to others and then starts fighting. As the matchstick burns itself before burning others. Exactly the same happens, when we get angry. Learn to get a hold of your tongue.

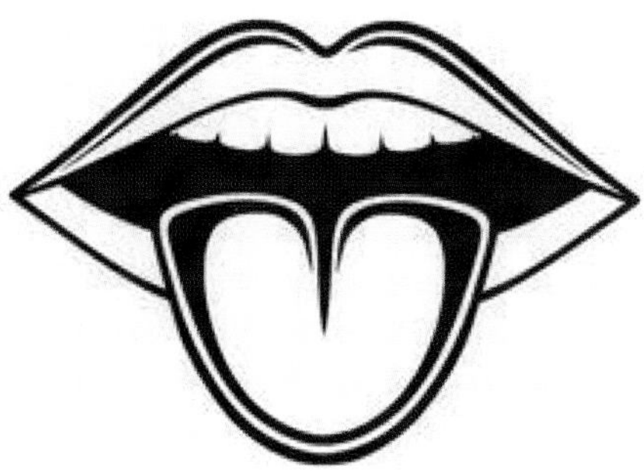

Once there was a quarrel between the teeth & the tongue. The teeth said that they work hard and she enjoys the taste. The tongue replied that only she knows how she manages to live among them. **"I send the food to you and at the end, I don't get anything and still you disturb me".** The teeth gave her warning that they would bite her.

After some time she noticed a wrestler coming to that side. She spoke to him in an abusive tone and went behind the teeth. The wrestler slapped and broke the teeth.

It is rightly said that the **"Tongue speaks abusive words and punishment is given to teeth and cheeks."**

According to Anekaantwaad excessive use of a thing or quality is harmful. Sometimes excessive speaking brings a lot of problems and the other time keeping quiet can embitter the relations. Keep good quality discussions in your relations for the healthy relations. It mostly happens that two strangers become friends only because of conversations. Later on, when they come close, they don't spend time together or talk to each other. They don't share minor things just like the earlier days. They do not enjoy small moments as they used to do earlier and they become indifferent to each other which can spoil the relation.

There may be some more reasons for this:

1. The burden of responsibilities is one of them.
2. He may be feeling much more mature and educated than earlier.
3. He may have become richer than earlier.
4. He may have the proud of his achievements.
5. He may be in poor economical or mental state.
6. He may not like carefree nature as he used to like.

If you are facing any of the above-mentioned situations, then get an alert. These may spoil your relations. Restart the things you used to do earlier like giving importance to small habits & issues. If one out of two does not do like this, then it will break the relationship. So there should be a good mutual understanding between the two you may feel yourself wiser and more experienced but still, have the conversation.

If you are not giving importance to the other one, or you are showing annoyance or you want to prove another one wrong, then it is sure, these habits are going to be the cause of bigger issue i.e. breaking of relationship

It's my humble advice to all that you may go very high in life but you should never give up a habit of sharing funs, jokes and everything. This is the best 'Mantra' i.e. secret of good, tension free life and strong relations. This is also called **"Vaatsalya Dharma of Samyakdrishti"**.

Means love your partner like a cow loves its calf. The calf runs to its mother again & again. And the calf also runs at the sound of its mother. And how the mother showers her affection when she meets the calf. But what can we say? Nowadays people turn away their faces or change their ways of seeing others. The selfless love among the people beautifies the value of the relations.

□

12 Contemplations

1. Your all kith and kin and your estate,
Mundane affluence and prestige level.
Everything exists like bubbles of water,
We all are beholder nothing stable.

2. We were alone at the time of birth,
We will be alone at the time of death.
None of my friend will go with me,
Besides my deeds and firm faith.

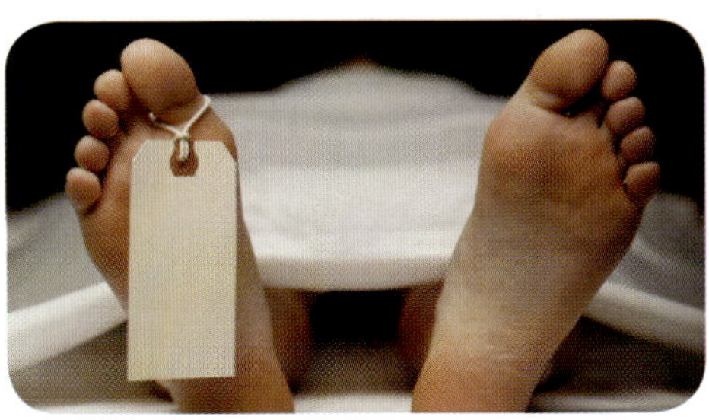

3. The poor are in sorrow in the lack of money,
Rich men are in grief to get more money.
There is no real pleasure in this world,
I have searched in the eye of every bird.

4. Every living being lives in relations,
None can provide you real protection.
What is your own thing at all,
At the time of death what you call.

5. Even your body is not yours,
How can other beings become yours?
Assets, family, and your home,
All are different daddy or mom.

6. Your body covered with thin skin,
So beautiful your's outlook.
Inside is blood bone and flesh,
Like this dirty no bad book.

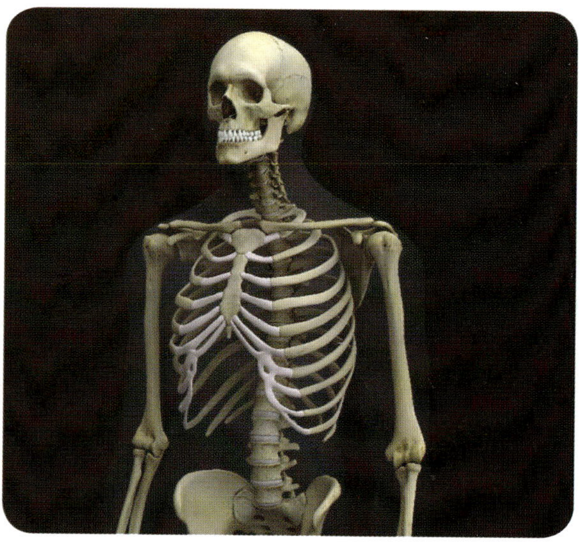

7. In the deep sleep of delusion,
All are wandering without vision.
Thieves of karmas exist everywhere,
No sense about them and not aware.

8. Deep sleep of delusion when breakdown,
Then one can listen to the precept of a noun.
Soul gets ways to rise upward,
Thieves of karmas fall downward.

9. Enlighten the lamp of knowledge with penance,
See your pure soul with clear sense.
To get rid of illusion is the only way,
Without it remains salvation away.

10. Accept five vows with great restraint,
Act carefully like a Digambar saint.
Very tough task to control five senses,
To eliminate karmas is this only process.

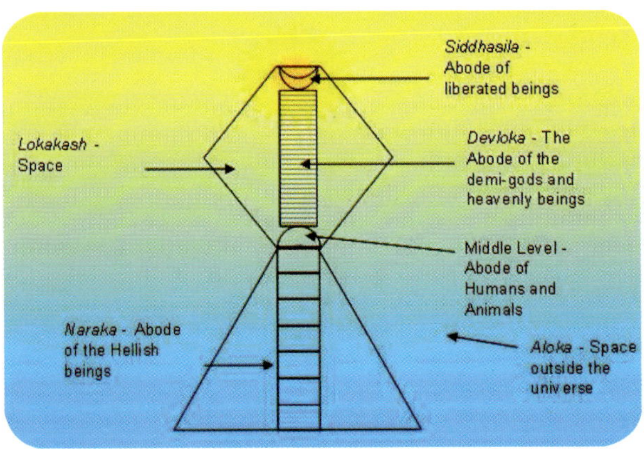

11. Money, gold, grain, kingdom, and happiness,
It can be achieved by easiness.
Most difficult to get in this universe,
Right faith, knowledge without any worse.

12. When we demand from divine tree,
And from Chintamani jewel we free.
But true religion gives everything,
Without any demand for anything.

Literature Writings by Digambar Muni Pranamya Sagar

Teeka Grantha in Sanskrit Language

- Lingapahud (Nandini Teeka)
- Sheelpahud (Nandini Teeka)
- Samadhi Tantra (Aarhatbhashya)
- Chetanya Chandrodaya (Chandrika Teeka)
- Barsanuvekkha (Kadambini Teeka)
- Aatma Anusasan (Swasti Teeka)
- Purushartha Sidduyapay (Mangla Teeka)
- Prasna Uttar Ratnamalika (Niti Path)
- Tatvartha Sutra (Tatva Sandipani Teeka)
- Sanskrit and Prakrit Bhakti (Aath Bhaktiyo Ki Tee-ka)

Anuvadit Granth in Hindi

- Satkarma Panjika
- Dus Bhakti Teeka
- Pravachan Sar (Saroj Bhaskar Teeka)
- Katha Kosh
- Satya Shasan Pariksha
- Yuktaynushasan
- Nammala (Bhasya)
- Satsankhyadi Anuyogdaur
- Patrakesri strotra
- Adhyastak Strotra

- Sanyas Ashostu Kimatmagatah
- Chaturvinsati Tirthankar Istuti (Aacharya Maghnandi)

Padhyanuvad

- Purushartha Siddhuyupay
- Prasnottar Ratan Malika
- Tatvarth Sutra
- Patra Kesri Strotra
- Kalyan Mandir Strotra
- Shri Vardhman Strotra
- Manglashtak
- Maghnandikrut Abhishek Path

In English

- Fact of Fate (articles)
- Twelve Contemplation
- I love my soul

Maulik Kavya in Sanskrit Language

- Istuti Pathah(In that)
  1. Prathana
  2. Veerastakam
  3. Bharatastakam,
  4. Shardastakum,
  5. Kundkundastakam,
  6. Samantabhadrastakam,
  7. Shantyastakam,
  8. Gyanastakam,
  9. Vidhyasatakam
  10. Maunasatkam
  11. Nijbodhastakam
  12. Aacharya Shri Gyan Sagar Prashati Patra
  13. Aacharya Shri Vidhyasagar Pujan
  14. Upyog Shatkam
- Shrayash pathah
- Siddhodayastakam

- Shri Vardhman Istrotam

Maulik Grantha in Prakrit Language

- Titthyar Bhavna (Solahkaran Bhavna Par Prakrit gathayan)
- Darshanik Pratikraman
- Anasakta Mahayogi (A complete lifestory of Acharya Shri Vidya Sagar Ji)
- Prakrit Shiksha - Part 1,2,3,4
- Asht Pahud Teeka
- Dhammkaha
- Prakrit Rachana Bhaskar

Anaya Maulik Krutiya

- Yugdrasta (Bhagwan Rishabh Dev Par Upanyas)
- Jain Samrat Chandra Gupt Maurya
- Khojo Mat Pao (Life Management)
- Alekh Path (20 Sedhantik Alekh)
- Samayasar Ka Gyani Atma Kaun?
- Aantargoonj (Bhajan and Haikoo)
- Lahar Par Lahar (Kavita Sangrah)
- Beta! (Shikshaprad Suktiya)
- Lakshya
- New Chahdhala
- Arham Dohavali
- Is Sallekhana/Santhara: A Suicide?

Sankalan

- Samvaad (Aacharya Shri and Baba Ramdev Ki Charcha)
- A Talk (English Translation of Samvaad)
- Purusharth Siddhyupay Anusheelan

□□□

ABOUT THIS BOOK

Place Of Writing	Place To Procure	Contact
Chaturmas 2017, Rewari	Aadi Submersibal And Pipe Store, Mall Godown Road Rewari (Haryana)	9416901501 9896521249 9671537209

Contribution in Publication	Cover & Text Design
Mr. Dinesh Jain & Mr. Arpit Jain, Rewari	SHUBHANGI JAIN, REWARI